INVISIBLE
IGUANAS
OF
ILLINOIS

Here's what readers from around the country are saying about Johnathan Rand's *AMERICAN CHILLERS:*

" I read THE MICHIGAN MEGA-MONSTERS in one day!"
Johnathan Rand's books are AWESOME!
-Ray M.., age 11, Michigan

"When I read FLORIDA FOG PHANTOMS, it really
creeped me out! What a great story!"
-Carmen T., age 11, Washington, D.C.

"Johnathan Rand's books are my favorite.
They're really creepy and scary!"
-Jeremy J., age 9, Illinois

"My whole class loves your books! I have two
of them and they are really, really cool."
-Katie R., age 12, California

"I never liked to read before, but now I read
all the time! The 'Chillers' series is great!"
-Lauren B., age 10, Ohio

"I love AMERICAN CHILLERS because they
are scary, but not too scary, because I don't want
to have nightmares."
-Adrian P., age 11, Maine

"I loved it when Johnathan Rand came to our
school. He was really funny. His books are great."
-Jennifer W., age 8, Michigan

"Johnathan Rand is my favorite author!"
-Kelly S., age 8, Michigan

"AMERICAN CHILLERS are great. I got one
for Christmas, and I loved it. Now, my sister
is reading it. When she's done, I'm going to
read it again."
-Joel F., age 13, New York

"I like the CHILLERS books because they are
fun to read. They are scary, too."
-Hannah K., age 11, Minnesota

"I read the MEGA-MONSTERS book and I
really liked it. Mr. Rand is a great writer."
-Ryan M., age 12, Arizona

"I LOVE AMERICAN CHILLERS!"
-Zachary R., age 8, Indiana

"I read your book to my little sister and
she got freaked out. I did, too!"
-Jason J., age 12, Ohio

"These books are my favorite! I love reading them!"
-Sarah N., age 10, New Jersey

"Your books are great. Please write more so I can read them.
-Dylan H., age 7, Tennessee

America's #1 Series for MAXIMUM Chills!

#6: Invisible Iguanas of Illinois

Johnathan Rand

An AudioCraft Publishing, Inc. book

Book storage and warehouses provided by Chillermania!©
Indian River, Michigan

Warehouse security provided by:
Lily Munster and Scooby-Boo

American Chillers #6: Invisible Iguanas of Illinois
ISBN 13-digit: 978-1-893699-30-4

Cover illustration by Dwayne Harris
Cover layout and design by Sue Harring

Invisible
Iguanas
of
Illinois

VISIT CHILLERMANIA!

WORLD HEADQUARTERS FOR BOOKS BY JOHNATHAN RAND!

Yooperland

Indian River

Alpena

Traverse City

MICHIGAN

CHILLERMANIA!

*I-75 Exit 313
then south
1 mile!*

Mt. Pleasant

Bay City

Grand Rapids

Lansing

Detroit

Kalamazoo

Visit the HOME for books by Johnathan Rand! Featuring books, hats, shirts, bookmarks and other cool stuff not available anywhere else in the world! Plus, watch the American Chillers website for news of special events and signings at *CHILLERMANIA!* with author Johnathan Rand! Located in northern lower Michigan, on I-75! Take exit 313 . . . then south 1 mile! For more info, call (231) 238-0338. And be afraid! Be veeeery afraaaaaaiiiid . . . .

1

When someone tells you a story, they usually start at the beginning.

And that's where I'm going to start. You have to know a couple of things before you can try to understand what has happened and why. And I will say this much:

What you are about to read is going to be pretty frightening at times. Not always, because there were some funny things that happened, too. But, for the most part, what my brother and I went through was pretty scary.

My name is Alyssa Barryton, and I'm eleven. I have a brother named Ryan. He's ten, but sometimes he doesn't act like it. Sometimes he acts like he's two!

We live in Springfield, Illinois. You've probably heard or read about our state, because Illinois is called the 'Land of Lincoln'. Abraham Lincoln called Illinois his home for over 30 years. In fact, if you ever come to Springfield, you can visit Abraham Lincoln's home. You'll see lots of really cool historical places.

But I doubt you'll see what I saw last year. Matter of fact, even I probably won't see it again.

I was walking to a friend's house after school. A group of us were going to meet and go for a bike ride along Lost Bridge Trail. It's a really cool paved path that's about five miles long. A lot of people jog, walk, and even rollerblade along the trail.

I stopped at a market that sells fresh fruits and vegetables and bought a small bag of radishes. That's right—radishes. I *love* radishes. I eat them raw, right out of the bag. I eat them the way most people eat candy.

I had just walked out the door and was opening the bag when I heard a noise from the alley next to the store. It was a swishing sound.

I turned and looked down the alley. The only thing I saw was a few garbage cans and a single parked car.

I didn't think anything of it, and I started to turn my head away.

And then:

I saw something.

Out of the corner of my eye, something had moved. Something had darted behind the garbage cans.

I stopped walking and scanned the alley to see what was there. The sun was shining, and the day was warm. It was the middle of June, and the summers can be pretty hot here in Springfield.

But I didn't see anything.

I pulled out a radish and popped it into my mouth.

Just an old alley cat, I thought, chewing on my radish.

Again, I turned and started to walk away, but I heard the noise again. It was the sound of something moving, shuffling across papers or leaves.

Once more, I glanced down the alley.

I stopped chewing.

What I saw wasn't a cat.

Or a dog.

Or a pigeon or a rabbit.

It was a tiny creature from outer space!

2

I blinked my eyes, and I realized what I was seeing wasn't a creature from outer space.

It was an *iguana!*

A lizard . . . a real, live iguana . . . was staring back at me! He was about a foot tall, and he was standing next to a garbage can! I could see his beady black eyes watching me.

Now, you have to understand something: Iguanas don't live in Illinois.

Period.

Oh, some people have them as pets, of course. And I saw a real big one at the Chicago Zoo.

But iguanas don't live in the wild.

Not in Illinois, they don't.

Which might explain why I thought that it was a creature from outer space!

The lizard turned his head. It was a bright green color, and it stood about as tall as a cat. Its tail made it look longer, though. And it had scales that began at the back of its head and went down the middle of its back. Its claws were long and sharp, like hooked nails.

Now, I didn't know anything about iguanas. I didn't know if they were vicious, or if they bit people. Who knows? Maybe they even *eat* people!

But I didn't think so. I don't think people would have them as pets if they ate humans.

I wanted to get closer so I could see the creature better. I took a real slow step, and then another.

The iguana didn't move. It just stood there, next to the garbage can, flashing his dark eyes at me.

Slowly, very slowly, I made my way down the

alley.

Closer . . . .

Closer . . . .

The iguana didn't move much. He turned his head a couple of times, but he continued eyeing me cautiously.

And it was really cool looking! I hadn't seen many iguanas before, except the one in the zoo. Now I was only a few feet away from one!

I stopped and held my breath. I kept expecting the creature to suddenly run off, to dart behind the garbage cans.

But it didn't.

It just stared at me.

I knelt down very slowly.

"Hey, buddy," I said sweetly. "Whatcha doin'?"

The lizard remained where he was.

"You're kind of cute," I said.

The iguana responded by opening his mouth.

Uh-oh, I thought. *Maybe he's getting mad.*

I had just started to stand back up when the lizard reared up, opened his mouth even wider,

and charged!
The iguana was attacking!

3

I didn't know what to do! I had never been
attacked by an iguana before!

And besides . . . I didn't have time to do
anything, anyway. In less than a second the
iguana had reached me.

I twisted to get out of the way, and in my
haste, I slipped, dropped my bag of
radishes — and fell.

I tumbled onto my back, and the lizard seized
the opportunity. He scrambled up my leg and
onto my stomach.

I was sure that this was the end for me.

Maybe iguanas eat people, after all.

I tried to scream, but no sound came out. My eyes were popping out of my head as the iguana came to a rest on my chest. His mouth was closed, but his black eyes were staring right into mine.

This was a nightmare. It had to be. I kept telling myself to wake up, to shake the dream away, but I couldn't.

And I could feel the lizard's heartbeat. His belly was pressed against my shirt, and I could actually feel his pounding heart going a mile a minute.

I took long, slow breaths. I didn't want the heaving of my chest to disturb the beast. It might make him even more mad.

The lizard turned his head, looking around. He blinked a few times.

"Help," I managed to say. But it was more of a squeak than anything, and besides . . . there was no one around to help, anyway.

"You're . . . you're not going to hurt me, are you," I said to the lizard. I know that it probably

was a silly thing to do, but hey . . . I didn't know what else to do.

When he heard my voice, he cocked his head to the side like a dog listening to a high-pitched sound.

Maybe it's friendly, I thought. *Maybe it's not mean, after all.*

I was wrong.

The iguana suddenly turned its head and stared directly into my eyes. He opened his mouth, and I could see rows and rows of teeth. They were really tiny—not like fangs or anything—but I knew that they were probably razor sharp.

And without warning, the vicious reptile lurched forward, mouth open and teeth bared. I could only watch in horror as the horrible lizard attacked, searching for the soft, tender flesh of my neck!

4

Talk about being freaked!

I was frozen in fear and I closed my eyes, waiting for the razor-sharp teeth to sink into my neck—

But the bite never came.

I had my eyes closed tightly, and I felt the iguana scramble up over my shoulder.

Then I heard a crunch, and I just knew that it was biting my ear.

But I didn't feel any pain!

Then I heard another crunch. And another. And then a chewing sound.

I opened my eyes and slowly turned my head.

The iguana was eating a radish! His jaw was going up and down, up and down, and he looked as happy as a clam!

Suddenly, I felt very foolish. I had been frightened by the creature . . . and all he wanted was a radish!

I scooched sideways and moved away from the lizard. It paid no attention. It just kept chewing on the radish.

"Hey," I said, "you're kinda cool." The iguana stretched out its neck and snared another radish.

Watching the creature and being so close at the same time was really awesome. Its skin was the color of summer leaves, and its eyes were the blackest of black.

And I began to wonder where it had come from. I didn't know a lot about iguanas, but I knew enough to know that they don't live in Illinois unless they're someone's pet.

That's it, I thought. *This must be someone's pet. I'll bet the little guy is friendly.*

It was risky, but I reached over and picked up the bag of radishes. The iguana was busy chewing on one, and it didn't do anything but continue chewing.

When it was done, I reached into the bag and pulled out another radish. I held it out.

The lizard took it! It ate right out of my hand!

This was really, really cool.

While he was chewing on the radish, I reached out again, very slowly, and touched the back of its head. The lizard instantly stopped chewing.

The iguana liked it! It liked being petted!

Then I began to wonder . . . just who does this creature belong to? Someone must be looking for it.

Gently . . . ever so gently . . . I picked up the creature and cradled it in my arms like a baby. It didn't seem to mind at all.

I looked around to see if anyone was looking for something.

Nope.

Then, I walked up the alley and looked

around. Cars sped by on the street, and there were a few people out walking around, but no one seemed to be looking for an iguana.

I walked back into the market and asked a woman at the service counter if anyone was missing an iguana.

That was a big mistake.

Now, I kind of figured that if anyone saw me carrying around an iguana in the store, they'd probably look twice. After all, it's not every day that you see a girl carrying a lizard around.

But when the woman at the service counter saw the lizard in my arms, she flipped out!

"Get that thing out of here this instant, young lady!" she ordered. *"This place sells food! We can't have ugly green snakes in here!"*

"It's not a snake," I replied. "It's an iguana."

"I don't care!" she snapped. "Get that disgusting creature out of the store!"

So, I had no choice but to take the lizard home. I figured that I could maybe make some signs and put them up around the neighborhood. Somewhere, someone was looking for their pet iguana. I just knew it.

Thankfully, Mom and Dad said that I could keep the reptile . . . but only until I found its owner. My brother Ryan thought that it was really cool, but he was a little afraid of it.

I called the pet store to find out how to take care of the iguana. Let me tell you . . . caring for an iguana is *nothing* like caring for a dog or a cat! An iguana takes a lot of hard work. I learned that they could be really great pets, but I also found out that they require a lot of attention. They really have a lot of special needs and require very unique care.

And that is how I came to have Iggy. Yep. You guessed it. I never found the owner. The man at the pet store said that some people don't realize how much work an iguana can be, and they just let them go to fend for themselves.

How horrible! Who could do such a thing?!?!

But if I thought *that* was horrible, it was *nothing* compared to the things that were about to happen.

And I will say this:

Prepare yourself. Because what was about to happen wasn't just *scary*.

It was *horrifying* . . . with a capital 'H'.

5

A month went by, and by now, I knew that Iggy was mine to keep.

I've said it before, and I'll say it again — having an iguana for a pet is a lot harder than having a dog or a cat.

Iguanas can't make their own body heat like us humans, so I had to make sure that he was always warm enough. I had to dig into my savings and buy a special light from the pet store. The light was kind of like a 'sun' for Iggy, so he could stay warm.

And he liked to climb on stuff. I had to spend

even more money on a big cage, and I put branches and a log inside of it.

But Iggy was fun to hang around with. Sometimes while I did my homework I would let him out of his cage and he would sit in the sunlight that came through my bedroom window.

Spooky wouldn't go near Iggy. He was freaked out. The first time Spooky saw Iggy, he ran and hid in Ryan's bedroom.

Even my brother, Ryan, who is afraid of just about everything, liked Iggy.

Summer ended and school began. I met a student in my class that had just moved here from Chicago . . . and he had *two* pet iguanas! One was named Jack, and the other was named Jill. The student's name was Stephen Jensen, and we became pretty good friends. He knew a lot about iguanas, and I learned a quite a bit from him.

After class one day he stopped me in the hallway.

"Hey, we're going on a vacation to Wisconsin next month," he said. "I don't have anyone to look after Jack and Jill. Do you think you could take care of them for a week?"

"You bet!" I said. "That would be cool!"

"I'll bring them over in their cage, just in case they don't get along with Iggy."

That's another thing I learned. Some iguanas don't get along well with other iguanas, and they'll fight like cats and dogs.

But I was sure that I wouldn't have any problem. Iggy is a really sweet creature, and I just knew that they'd get along well.

Well, as it turned out, Iggy and Jack and Jill weren't going to get along. They didn't like each other *at all*.

But that wasn't the problem.

The problem was something altogether different, and it began the night that my brother Ryan opened up a package that was sent to him in the mail.

6

Stephen had brought Jack and Jill over, and, unfortunately, they began hissing at one another in their cages. Jack and Jill didn't even want to be in the same room with Iggy!

I asked Ryan if he could keep Jack and Jill in his room. I would take care of them and feed them and give them fresh water, I said.

Surprisingly, Ryan said that it would be okay. I was surprised because usually my brother doesn't want me anywhere *near* his room.

"Hey, what's that?" I asked him. There was a brown package on his dresser that was addressed to him. The top was opened, and it was stuffed with bubble wrap.

"Oh, it came in the mail," he said. "I ordered it from the back of one of my comic books. It's a powder that is supposed to make you invisible."

"What?!?!" I exclaimed.

"That's what it says. See for yourself."

"That's ridiculous!" I said. "You got ripped off."

He shrugged. "Well, I figured it was worth a try," he said.

I pulled out some of the bubble wrap and, sure enough, there was a small bag that had a label on the side that read 'invisibility powder'. The bag was clear, and it contained a brown-colored dusty substance.

"This is a joke, right?" I asked.

"Hey, I don't know," he said. "I haven't tried it yet. But I thought it would be cool if it worked."

That's my brother for you. He's always wasting his money on silly things.

"I'll be back to check on the iguanas in a little

while," I said.

"Fine with me," Ryan said. "I'm going to do my homework."

Well, that was my first mistake. I should have never left my brother alone with Stephen's two iguanas. I should have known that he would have been curious, and would want to pet the lizards.

When I returned to check on the lizards, Ryan was gone. On the dresser, the bag of powder had been opened, and some of it had spilled out.

I shook my head and smiled. *Ryan is so weird,* I thought.

I knelt down on the floor and peered into the lizard cage. Jack and Jill were lying next to each other on a big branch.

"How are you guys?" I said.

One of the reptiles turned and looked at me. Both of the creatures looked bored.

"I'll take you guys out for a walk in a little while," I said. I stood up.

"Hey Alyssa," I heard Ryan say. I turned around.

He wasn't there!

"What?" I asked. He must be in the hall.

"It works!" I heard him exclaim.

But I couldn't see him!

"Where are you?" I asked.

"I'm right here!" he said. "The invisibility powder! It really, really works!"

I gasped. I could hear Ryan's voice. He was here, in the room—but I couldn't see him!

Ryan was invisible!

7

"Oh my gosh!" I gasped, covering my mouth with my hands. Ryan was nowhere to be seen . . . but I had heard his voice!

"It works!" I heard Ryan say.

But something wasn't quite right, and I grew suspicious.

"Say something again," I said curiously.

"Something again," he mocked.

Suddenly, his bedroom door creaked open.

"You goofball!" I exclaimed. "You're not invisible!"

"I never said I was," he replied with a sly grin

on his face. "You heard my voice and thought that I had vanished."

I shook my head. *Brothers,* I thought. *Brothers are nothing but trouble.*

"I'm going to try the invisibility powder later tonight," Ryan said. "Then we'll see if it'll work."

"It's a gimmick," I said, shaking my head. "You got ripped off. There's no way a silly powder is going to make you invisible."

"*Alyssa! Ryan!*" I heard Mom call from the kitchen. "*Time for dinner!*"

We had chicken and corn on the cob . . . my favorite. All through dinner, Ryan kept talking about his new invisibility powder, and how he was going to use it. Dad said that if it worked, *he* wanted to borrow it, too. Mom just rolled her eyes.

After dinner we helped with the dishes. Ryan complained about it, as usual, but he helped anyway. All he could do was talk about how cool it was going to be to vanish and become invisible.

"Are you going to watch?" he said, as we finished up the dishes. He dried his hands with a towel, then handed it to me.

"Yeah," I said. "I'm going to watch you make a fool of yourself."

I followed him down the hall and into his bedroom.

"I'm telling you," he said, "this is going to be cool. I can't wait to go to school and be invisible! I'll be able to sneak in the lunch line and get extra snacks!"

I shook my head again. "Okay, Mr. Magician," I said. "Let's see you do your stuff."

Ryan walked to his dresser, but he stopped abruptly and turned.

"Wait a minute," he said, looking down. He pointed. "Aren't they supposed to be in the cage?"

I looked down.

The door to the cage that was supposed to hold Jack and Jill was open! And what was worse . . . the two iguanas were gone!

"Oh no!" I exclaimed. My eyes darted around the room. "They got out!"

I dropped down onto my hands and knees

and looked under Ryan's bed.

Nothing.

"They have to be close by," I said frantically. "They couldn't have—"

"Uh-oh," Ryan interrupted. I didn't like the sound of his voice, either. He sounded worried.

"What is it?" I asked, getting to my feet.

Ryan was standing at his dresser, holding an empty bag.

"My invisibility powder!" he shrieked. *"It's gone! Those two little buggers ate my invisibility powder!"*

"Quick!" I exclaimed. "We have to find them fast!"

Ryan and I began scurrying around the room, and another horrifying thought came to me.

"*Stop!*" I yelled suddenly, and Ryan froze and looked at me.

"What?" he asked.

"If Jack and Jill are invisible, we won't be able to see them! We might step on them by accident!"

Ryan looked down.

"Yeah, that probably wouldn't be good. Geez! I can't believe those two things ate my invisibility powder!"

"I can't believe the stuff worked," I said.

"Well, if we can't move around, how are we going to find them?" he asked.

"Very carefully," I replied. I slowly lowered myself to the floor and began sweeping my hands along the carpet. When I didn't feel one of the iguanas, I crouched down on all fours. Ryan did the same.

"We're going to have to move like this until we find them," I said.

"*If* we find them," Ryan replied.

"We *have* to find them," I insisted. "Stephen is counting on me to take care of them."

"A fine job you did," Ryan said, sweeping his hands over the floor. "What's he going to say when you hand him a cage with nothing in it? Even if you find them, what good are two invisible iguanas?"

He was right, of course. But I'd figure that out later. Right now, all I wanted to do was get my hands on those two iguanas . . . whether they were invisible or not!

We went over the room carefully. We probably looked pretty silly, moving real slow, sweeping our hands over the carpet and the bed. I just knew that my hands would suddenly touch something that I couldn't see, and we'd find the iguanas.

But we didn't.

"I can't believe a company would sell *real* powder that would make you invisible!" I said. I was getting more and more frustrated by the moment.

"I can't believe those green reptiles ate all of the stuff," Ryan replied. "That powder cost me four bucks! You're going to have to buy me some more, you know," he finished.

"Would you be quiet and help me find these things?!?!" I demanded. "If we don't find them fast, they could get hurt. How long will they stay invisible?"

"Beats me," Ryan said. "I didn't read the directions."

"You mean, you were going to try the invisibility powder on yourself, and you don't

43

even know how it works?"

"Well, hey . . . I bought it from an ad in my comic book. It has to be pretty safe."

"Well, a fine mess we're in now," I exclaimed. "I just know that something awful is going to happen any minute."

And it did . . . starting with a terrible scream from the living room!

9

The scream made Ryan and I jump.

"That's Mom!" I shouted. Ryan sprang to his feet.

"Be careful!" I reminded him. Then I got up and dashed out of the bedroom behind him.

I needn't have worried. We sprang down the hall to see Mom backed up against the living room wall — and Jack and Jill were on the floor!

I heaved a huge sigh of relief. Jack and Jill were safe!

"Come . . . and . . . get . . . these . . . *things!*" Mom ordered.

"They're just iguanas," I said, bounding down the hall and into the living room. "They got out of their cage."

"I don't care," Mom said. "If you can't keep them in their cage, they're going to have to go somewhere else!"

Gulp.

"That would be a bummer," I whispered.

"Yeah," Ryan said. "And they're not even invisible." He sounded disappointed.

"I told you that it wouldn't work," I said. "They must have gotten out of their cage on their own."

"Maybe they *were* invisible, but it wore off," Ryan pondered.

I carefully picked up an iguana in each hand, and began walking back down the hall to put them back into the cage.

But then I had another horrible thought. *What if the powder made the iguanas sick?* It was obvious that the iguanas had eaten the powder. While I was sure that it hadn't made them invisible . . . what would happen if the creatures got sick from it?

I put Jack and Jill into their cage, shut the door, and double-checked to make sure it was shut tight. I didn't want them getting out again.

Then I went straight for the phone and called the pet store.

"I know this is going to seem like a silly question," I began, "but I have two iguanas that ate invisibility powder. Do you think they might get sick?"

There was a long pause, and then the woman at the pet store answered. "They ate *what?*"

"Invisibility powder," I replied. "My brother ordered it through—"

I was interrupted by a flurry of laughter. Then there was a click, and the line went dead.

"Hello?" I said. "Hello? Mrs. Pet Shop Lady? Hello?"

Rats.

As it turned out, I had good reason to be afraid. Oh, not because Jack and Jill had eaten Ryan's invisibility powder.

No, there were things that were about to

happen that were far worse than sick iguanas.

And it all began that night, after dark, after I went to bed . . . .

I got to stay up late that night, which was pretty cool. We watched a movie on TV and ate popcorn. During the commercials I went into Ryan's room to check on Jack and Jill. They seemed to be fine. I don't know just what was in the powder that they ate, but it didn't seem to bother them.

Which was a good thing. I couldn't stand the thought of the two creatures getting sick . . . or worse. And how would I explain it to Stephen?

I checked on Iggy, too. I was worried that maybe he had somehow eaten some of the strange powder, and would be invisible. Thankfully, he was fine.

I walked back into the living room and watched the rest of the movie. Then I went to bed and fell asleep.

But not for long.

First of all, I kept having dreams about invisible iguanas. Weird! Every so often I would wake up. Once, I clicked on the light to find Iggy staring back at me.

"Glad to see you, buddy" I whispered groggily. *"I'm glad you haven't vanished."* Iggy just blinked. I turned off the light and fell back to sleep.

Later, I was awakened by a noise. A creaking sound. I turned to see my bedroom door opening slowly. It was a little spooky, but then I heard my brother's voice.

"Alyssa? Are you sleeping?"

"Yes," I replied. *"I'm sound asleep. Leave me alone."*

He clicked the light on, and I squinted in the bright light. *"Hey!"* I hissed. *"Shut that off! Go back to bed!"* I pulled the sheets over my head and turned away.

"Jack and Jill are gone again," Ryan said with alarm.

That got my attention.

I pulled the sheets down and turned. *"What?!?!"* I exclaimed, leaping out of bed.

"They're gone," Ryan explained frantically. "I heard strange noises, and when I turned on the light, the cage was open. I didn't do it, honest. I looked all over my room, but I didn't find Jack or Jill."

"We've got to find them before Mom does," I said. "If they keep getting loose, she's going to make me take them somewhere else."

Ryan turned and I followed him down the hall to his bedroom.

"How are they getting out of their cage?" I whispered.

Ryan shrugged. "Got me," he said.

My attention was diverted to a movement under Ryan's bed.

"There's one of them, right there," I said, falling to my knees. "I just saw him."

I leaned over and peered under the bed . . . and gasped.

It was then that I knew that my iguana babysitting adventure was about to turn into a nightmare.

It was Jack . . . or Jill . . . one of the two. But something strange was happening.

I reached under the bed to try and pull him out, but he wriggled away.

What's more, he became harder and harder to see . . . like he was dissolving.

And, in fact, he was! *He was vanishing!*

I gasped and rubbed my eyes. "I must be dreaming," I said. "I must be still asleep."

"What's the matter?" Ryan asked, dropping to his knees. He peered under the bed.

"Look!" I said, pointing at the iguana.

"What's . . . what's happening to him?" Ryan stammered.

"It . . . it looks like he's disappearing!" I exclaimed.

"Cool!" Ryan replied. "See? The invisibility powder works, after all!"

"So what?!?" I said. "If this thing disappears, we're in big trouble!"

"You'd better grab him quick, or you'll never find him!" Ryan said.

Ryan had a point. It would be almost impossible to find an invisible iguana. How would we go about trying to find something that wasn't visible?

By now, the iguana was almost completely invisible. He was fading away like green smoke.

I reached out quickly, and was surprised when I felt the body of the iguana in my hands.

"I've . . . I've got him!" I said, slowly pulling the creature from beneath the bed.

"Do you really?" Ryan said in wonder. "I can't see him!"

"I have him," I said. "And he's invisible, all

right!"

It sure was a weird feeling holding onto something that you can't see. The iguana wasn't really big, maybe a couple pounds or so, but it was really strange knowing that I held a living creature in my hands that I couldn't see!

I stood up, cradling the invisible reptile in my arms. I would have to be careful while I was holding him, otherwise he might get hurt.

"Let me touch him," Ryan said, and he reached out with his hand. He was surprised when he could feel the skin of the lizard.

"That's crazy!" he exclaimed, as he gently stroked the iguana.

"Now we have another problem," I said.

"What's that?"

"Where's the other one?" I asked.

We both looked around the room.

"Maybe it's already invisible," Ryan said.

The iguana that I was cradling in my arms squirmed and shifted.

"Is that Jack or Jill?" Ryan asked.

"I can't tell," I replied. "I can't see it."

"Well, duh," Ryan said with a bite. "I just wanted to know who I should call."

"It doesn't matter. I don't think iguanas will come when they're called."

The creature shifted in my arms again, but then I noticed something: it felt *heavier.*

A *lot* heavier.

And *bigger.*

"What on earth . . . ." I said.

"What?" Ryan asked. "What is it?"

"I . . . I don't know," I replied. "But . . . this thing is getting . . . heavy. And . . . and it's getting bigger!"

By now, it was so heavy that I had to struggle to hold on. My arms were spread wide as I tried to hold onto the creature.

Suddenly, I couldn't hold on any longer, and I let go. But it didn't fall. It must have grown so big that it could touch the floor!

Oh no! Not only was the iguana invisible . . . *but now it had grown to ten times its normal size!*

12

There was no way we were staying in his bedroom a moment longer. There were too many freaky things happening, too much strange stuff going on.

So Ryan and I did the only thing we could.

We ran.

I bolted out his door with my brother right behind me. My thoughts whirled and raced.

How can this be happening? I wondered as I headed down the hall. *How can iguanas become invisible? And how can they grow to ten times their own size?!?!*

There is a big closet in the hallway, and the door was open. We would be safe in there . . . at least for now, until we found out what was going on.

I was the first in the closet, with Ryan right behind me. All of a sudden he was yanked away from the closet door, and sent sprawling down the hall!

"It's got me!" he shrieked. *"The thing's got me! Help, Alyssa! Help me!"*

This was worse than a nightmare . . . it was a catastrophe! Ryan was being dragged away, kicking and screaming, by a giant invisible iguana!

I couldn't just stand by and do nothing, so I leapt from the closet and charged down the hall. I reached Ryan and grabbed his arm.

"He's got the collar of my pajamas!" he shrieked.

I pulled with all my might . . . and Ryan suddenly tumbled forward.

"Back to the closet!" I yelled, and we sprang down the hall. This time, I pushed Ryan in first, then I jumped in behind him and pulled the door closed.

"Oh my gosh!" he panted. Both of us were out of breath, and our hearts were beating a mile a minute.

"We have to get Mom and Dad!" I whispered. *"We have to warn them!"*

"We can't leave the closet!" Ryan gasped. *"We'll be eaten by those giant lizards!"*

Ryan was right. We didn't know enough about the giant invisible iguanas.

But one thing we *did* know . . . they didn't appear to be friendly. Not anymore, they didn't.

And we were trapped. Oh, sure, we were safe, at least for the time being . . . but we were stuck in this closet.

Then—

Scrit scrit scrit.

Ryan and I jumped, and we backed away from the door as far as we could. It was dark, and there wasn't even a light to turn on . . . which made everything even *more* scary.

The scratching came again.

Scrit scrit scrit.

"He's trying to get us!" Ryan hissed.

Scrit scrit scrit . . . Scrit scrit scrit.

"Shhhhhh!" I replied as quietly as I could. *"Maybe he doesn't know we're here! Maybe he'll go away!"*

"I hope so," Ryan said quietly. *"I don't want to be eaten by that thing!"*

"Neither do I!" I answered.

The scratching stopped, and all we could hear was the pounding of our hearts. Then we could hear shuffling.

"He's leaving!" Ryan cried out quietly.

"Shhhh!" I told him.

We waited and waited. I was too terrified to move, too frightened to do anything . . . but we couldn't stay in the closet all night!

"Go and get Mom and Dad," I ordered Ryan.

"Say *what?!?!?!*" Ryan protested. "I'm not going anywhere! Not with the Jolly Green Monsters waiting for us!"

"Don't be a chicken," I said.

"You're older than me," Ryan reminded me. "You're supposed to watch over me. *You* go get Mom and Dad!"

Ryan was right. I was the older sister, and I

should be watching out for my kid brother.

Reluctantly, I agreed to go. I would open up the closet door, make sure the coast was clear, and then run down the hall and downstairs to Mom and Dad's room.

Wait a minute, I thought. *How will I know if the coast is clear? The iguanas are invisible!*

It was a chance that I would have to take. If we didn't want to spend the night in the closet, *someone* was going to have to go and get Mom and Dad.

Besides . . . Mom and Dad might be in danger, themselves. And what if the iguanas were already there? Would the creatures be after Mom and Dad like they were after us?

Regardless, it was a chance I would have to take.

"Okay," I said quietly to Ryan. "I'll go. You stay here, in the closet, where it's safe. I'll go and get Mom and Dad."

"Be careful," Ryan said.

In the darkness, I found the doorknob.

Here goes nothing, I thought, as I turned the

knob and pushed the door open. *I hope you're making the the right decision.*

The door opened, and I was about to step out into the hall . . . when I realized I hadn't made the right decision.

I had made the worst possible decision of all—and I knew it the moment I felt the terrible claws grab tightly around my wrist.

13

I screamed like I had never screamed before in my life. I wanted to scream so loud that Mom and Dad heard it. I wanted the neighbors to hear it. I wanted everyone on our block to hear it!

The strong claw held fast to my hand and started to pull.

"Ryan!" I screeched. *"It's got me! It's got me!"* In the darkness, I reached for him. He found my free hand and grabbed hold, and began pulling.

"What in the world are you doing in this closet?!?!?" a gruff voice demanded, and I felt a surge of relief rocket through my body.

Dad!

I leapt out of the closet and into the hall. I was so happy to see him that I wrapped my arms around his waist.

"You saved us!" I exclaimed. "You saved us!"

Ryan stumbled forward and emerged from the closet.

"Saved you from what?" Dad asked. He sounded angry.

"From the giant invisible iguanas!" Ryan replied. "They're huge!"

Dad drew back and put his hands on his hips. "What are you talking about?" he demanded. I knew right away that it was going to be pretty hard to get him to believe us.

"He's not lying, honest," I said, nodding my head. "One of the iguanas vanished right in my arms. Then he grew gigantic, and tried to run off with Ryan!"

"Uh-huh," Dad said. "Invisible iguanas. Now I've seen everything."

"No, you can't see them," Ryan said. "They're invisible!"

"Both of you go back to your rooms. *Now.*" His voice was strong and angry. "And I don't want to find you playing in this closet again. Especially in the middle of the night."

"But . . . but—"

"No but's about it," Dad said, shaking his head, and I knew that it was pointless to argue with him.

"All right," Ryan said to Dad. "I'll go back to bed . . . but I want *you* to come to my bedroom to make sure that there's nothing there waiting to eat me."

"Me too," I chimed in.

"You guys are out of your minds!" Dad exclaimed. "There are no such things as invisible iguanas!"

Regardless, Dad followed me to my bedroom and waited while I walked all around. Iggy was still in his cage, and he stared at me blankly as I swept my arms around beneath my bed, in my closet, and all over the room. All the while, Dad shook his head. He thought I was nuts!

Satisfied, I leapt into bed and pulled the

covers up to my chin. "Close the door!" I said.

Dad shook his head as he closed the door, and I heard him walk away as he followed Ryan to his room. I pulled the covers over my head and trembled. There was nothing I could do but *hope* that there would be no more iguana attacks tonight.

Tomorrow, I thought. *Tomorrow we'll get it all figured out. Tomorrow we'll find out what's going on.*

Oh, we'd find out all right. We'd find out *exactly* what was going on. Up until now, things were just weird and creepy. Oh, things had been a little scary, sure.

But things were about to get a lot scarier. Scarier—and *dangerous,* with a capital 'D' . . . .

14

I was awakened in the morning by a knock on my bedroom door. It opened, and Ryan poked his head in.

"Alyssa? Are you asleep?"

"Yes," I replied. "Leave me alone."

Suddenly, I remembered the events during the night. I rolled sideways and sat up. "Did you find Jack and Jill?" I asked.

Ryan shook his head. "I woke up, and I thought that I dreamed everything," he said. "Then I looked over at the cage. Both of the iguanas were still gone."

"We weren't dreaming," I said. "We both couldn't have had the same dream."

"I'll say," Ryan said. "If you were in my dream, I would have kicked you out."

"We've got to find out what's going on," I said, ignoring his comment. "Iguanas can't just *disappear*."

"Jack and Jill did," Ryan replied. "And they're still gone."

"Well, it's no use trying to explain to Mom and Dad," I said. "Dad already thinks we're crazy. And he's probably mad at us, too. We're lucky we didn't get grounded for telling a fib."

"But we weren't *telling* a fib," Ryan replied. "We were *telling* the *truth*."

"*I* know that, and *you* know that," I said. "But *Dad* doesn't know that. He thinks we were just clowning around. If we're going to figure out what's going on around here, it's going to be up to you and me."

During breakfast, Dad didn't say anything about the things that happened the night before. He finished his eggs and went to work, just like he always does. Ryan and I helped clean up the kitchen, and then we both went to pick up our room.

"Alyssa?" Mom called from the living room.

I went to the top of the stairs. "Yes?" I called down.

"What do you know about this?" she asked.

I walked out of my bedroom, down the hall, and stopped at the top of the stairs. Mom was in the living room, standing near the television. A large plant in a big pot sat next to the TV, and she was looking at it curiously.

"What?" I asked, walking toward her.

"This," she replied, taking one of the leaves in her hand. "Look."

There was a large bite mark taken out of the leaf! Something had eaten part of it!

I shrugged. "Gee, Mom . . . I don't know."

She inspected the leaf carefully. "The bite in the leaf is too big to be from an iguana," she said, "otherwise, that would be my first guess."

Mom was right: the bite out of the leaf *was*

big. But then again, she didn't know what Ryan and I knew about Jack and Jill.

"Is the plant going to die?" I asked.

"I don't think so," Mom replied, shaking her head. She let go of the leaf, and it hung limp. "It sure is strange, though." She turned and looked at the clock on the wall. "Oh, my!" she exclaimed. "It's nearly ten o'clock! I'm going to be late for work!" And with that, she scurried off. "Be sure to finish picking up your room," she called out as she went out the front door. "And remind your brother, too! Lunch is in the fridge."

"Thanks, Mom," I shouted just before the front door closed.

I went back upstairs to Ryan's room, and told him about the bite that Mom discovered in the leaf.

"Good thing that iguana didn't take a bite out of you or me," he said. Then he looked at me, and I could see the fear in his eyes. "What are we going to do?" he asked.

"We're going to call the company you ordered that invisibility powder from, that's what we're going to do," I said. "Maybe they can help."

"Good idea," he agreed. He walked over to his dresser, picked up a comic book, and flipped it open. "Here is the ad, right here," he said. "And look . . . it's even a free call!"

We went downstairs and I picked up the phone. Ryan gave me his comic book, and I dialed the number. After a few rings, someone answered.

"Goofy Stuff, Incorporated," a male voice said. "How may I help you?"

"Um . . . yes," I answered. I was a bit nervous. "My . . . my brother ordered some invisibility powder from you guys, and it works great. But how do you reverse it?"

"It's all in the instructions," the voice responded coldly.

I looked at Ryan and put my hand over the telephone mouthpiece. *"He said that it's in the instructions,"* I whispered.

"I threw them away," he whispered back.

"You WHAT?!?!?" I hissed back.

Ryan shrugged. *"Well . . . I didn't think I'd need*

them."

"Um . . . I'm sorry, but we don't have the instructions," I explained to the man on the phone.

"Well, you should always read and keep the instructions," he replied with a hint of anger in his voice.

"Please, mister . . . I'm sorry we don't have the instructions, but we really need to know how to make things visible again."

He sighed. "It's very simple. Just sprinkle some baking soda on whatever it is that you made vanish. It will reappear instantly."

I breathed a sigh of relief, and the man continued.

"You don't need a lot of baking soda, either," he said. "Just a little. Of course, it doesn't work on reptiles, but I'm sure you read that in the directions."

Uh-oh.

"What . . . what do you mean *'it doesn't work on reptiles'*?" I asked.

"Oh, yes. Under no circumstance should you

use the invisibility powder to make reptiles vanish. It does nasty things to them."

"N . . .n . . . nasty things?" I stammered.

"Awful things," the man confirmed. "Why, we had a boy that called here once. He said he'd made his snake disappear. Next thing you know, it was forty feet long. It ate a car and a tree."

"A car and a tree?!?!?" I exclaimed.

"Oh, yes. Once you make a reptile invisible, there's no telling what might happen."

Oh my gosh!

"Thank you for your help," I said, my voice trembling.

I hung up the phone to give Ryan the bad news . . . but I didn't have time.

Outside, from our next door neighbors house, we heard a terrible scream.

"Oh my!! Ahhhh! Someone stop him! Stop him before it's too late!"

The neighborhood was about to be turned into a madhouse.

15

Ryan and I sprang into action. He was the first to reach the front door, and he threw it open and leapt outside. I followed on his heels, and we both dashed off the porch and sprinted into the yard.

Next door, Mrs. O'Malley was standing by the hedge. Her hands were on her cheeks and her eyes were wide with horror. She was looking at something in her yard, but we couldn't see what it was.

I ran up to the hedge, and Ryan followed.

"What's the matter, Mrs. O'Malley?" I asked.

"It's awful!" she cried, and then she covered her eyes with her hands. "Oh, I just can't bear to look!"

Ryan and I peered over the hedge.

"Oh, for crying out loud," he whispered.

At the end of her yard, near the sidewalk, a big, black dog was eating Mrs. O'Malley's flowers! He was standing in the middle of the garden, chewing on flower tops like they were biscuits!

"That's only Sammy!" I explained. "He belongs to a friend of ours. He won't hurt you."

"He's eating all of my flowers!" Mrs. O'Malley cried. "How horrible! How terribly, terribly *horrible!*"

Ryan walked along the hedge and into Mrs. O'Malley's yard. "Hey Sammy!" he said. "Here boy! Come here!"

Hearing his name, Sammy wagged his tail happily and bounded out of the garden. He ran up to Ryan.

"Sit."

Sammy obeyed, and Ryan patted the dog's

head. "Good boy, Sammy. Good boy."

"We'll take him for you," I told Mrs. O'Malley. "I know who he belongs to."

"Oh, my poor, poor flowers," Mrs. O'Malley said.

"Well, it doesn't look like he ate *too* many," I said, trying to sound hopeful.

Mrs. O'Malley walked over to her garden. I followed along the side of the hedge until I came to the sidewalk, then I strode over to her garden.

"Yes, I guess you're right," Mrs. O'Malley said. "It looks like he only ate a few."

I was glad. I didn't want Sammy to get into trouble!

"We'll take him home for you," I told her again. "I don't think you'll have to worry about Sammy eating your flowers again."

Mrs. O'Malley returned to her house, and I walked up to Ryan.

"Bad dog," I told Sammy, but I didn't scold him too hard. He was just being a dog.

"Come on," I said to Ryan. "Let's get him home."

I began walking away, but Ryan didn't move. He acted like he hadn't even heard me.

"Ryan?" I called back to him. "Come on . . . we have problems of our own to figure out."

Ryan still didn't move. Both he and Sammy were looking at Mrs. O'Malley's flower garden.

"What . . . what is it?" I asked, walking back up to him.

Slowly, Ryan raised his hand, and it was then that I saw the expression of fear on his face.

"L . . . l . . . look," he stammered.

I stared at where he was pointing, and I couldn't believe what I was seeing!

Flowers were disappearing right before our eyes! They were vanishing into thin air like . . . like something was eating them!

And right away, I knew what it was. There was only one thing that it could possibly be:

One of the invisible iguanas!

16

"Are you not seeing what I'm not seeing?" Ryan asked quietly.

"I'm not seeing anything," I replied, "except flowers vanishing into thin—"

"*Listen!*" Ryan hissed, interrupting me. I stopped speaking and listened intently. At first, I couldn't hear anything besides the things we normally hear in our neighborhood: birds, shouts from kids on the other block, and the hum of cars on the highway several blocks away. But then:

Chewing! I could hear a chewing sound!

Suddenly, Sammy started growling. The hair

on his back raised up, and his tail went stiff. Whatever was going on, the dog didn't like it, either.

"It's . . . it's got to be one of . . . of them!" I said. "One of the invisible iguanas!"

Without warning, Sammy suddenly stopped growling. His tail went between his legs, and he turned and sprinted off down the street without looking back. Whatever was going on, he'd been pretty scared.

"Let's go get some baking soda!" I said. "Quick!"

Ryan shook his head. "You told me the guy on the phone said that it didn't work on reptiles," he said.

Is that what he said? I wondered. Now that I thought about it, I didn't remember. I know that he had told me that we shouldn't put the invisibility powder on reptiles . . . but I don't think he said anything about putting baking soda on them.

"Let's go call them again," I said. "Just to be safe."

We ran into the house. Ryan retrieved his comic book again, and I dialed the number ... but I got a busy signal.

I tried again. Still busy.

Ryan shook his head. "We're going to run out of time," he said. "That iguana is going to eat all of Mrs. O'Malley's flowers!"

"Let's call the police," I said. "We shouldn't be handling something like this."

"Yeah, but it's our fault in the first place! They'll take us to jail!"

I thought about it for a moment. "Well, maybe so," I began, "but what if those iguanas wind up hurting someone?"

I picked up the phone and dialed the number for the police. I gave the man who answered my name and my address, and then I told him what was wrong.

"That's right, sir. Iguanas. Giant ones. They're invisible. They're invisible and they—"

I was suddenly interrupted by thunderous laughter.

"Ooh, that's a good one!" the policeman said.

"Giant invisible iguanas terrorizing Springfield! Now *that's* funny!"

There was a click, and the phone went dead. I placed the telephone receiver on the table.

"No one is going to believe us," I said. "It's just too crazy."

"Try the company again," Ryan urged.

I called Goofy Stuff, Incorporated, but the line was still busy.

"We can't wait any longer," I said. "We've got to stop the iguanas before something terrible happens. I'll get the baking soda."

Mom keeps a small box of baking soda in the refrigerator. She says that it helps keep everything fresh. I found it on the bottom shelf and poured a little bit of the fine powder into my hand.

"You mean, that's *it?*" Ryan asked.

"I guess so," I said. "The man said that it only takes a little."

"Let's take the whole box, just to be safe," he said. "Come on."

We rushed back outside and over to the

hedge. I could still see flowers disappearing, and I could hear chomping. I was sure that one—or *both*—of the iguanas were still there.

"Here," I said, handing the box of baking soda to Ryan. "Go up there and toss some powder around."

"Me?!?!" Ryan protested. "Why me?!?!"

"Because you're the one who left the invisibility powder where the iguanas could eat it," I said.

"Yeah, well you're the one that was babysitting the two iguanas," he said.

I shook my head. "Sorry," I said. "You're not off the hook this time. It was *your* invisibility powder that made this happen."

"All right," Ryan said. "We'll both do it. But how are we going to put baking soda on something we can't see?"

"We'll get close to the garden and toss the baking soda into the air. Hopefully, some of it will land on the iguana."

"I hope this works," Ryan said.

At the garden, the flowers were still

disappearing.

"Let's go," I said, "before the thing chomps all of Mrs. O'Malley's flowers."

We walked around the hedge and onto the sidewalk, then strode into Mrs. O'Malley's yard. I wondered if the iguana could see us. Probably.

And, I have to admit, I was a little afraid. After all, there's no telling what a giant invisible iguana might do.

We reached the flower garden. Ryan was still holding the box of baking soda.

"Go ahead," I said. "Take a handful and throw it in the air."

Ryan turned the box on its side and dumped a small pile of white baking soda into his hand.

"Here goes nothing," he said, and with that, he swept his arm out. The baking powder filled the air for a moment, then began falling. Some of it landed on the flowers and on the leaves. Still more of it landed on the ground.

Suddenly, the chomping sounds stopped. Without warning, a loud shriek came from out of nowhere.

I cupped my hands over my ears. Ryan dropped the box of baking soda to the ground, where it spilled all over the grass. Then he placed his hands over his ears, too.

As it turned out, Ryan had covered the invisible iguana with baking soda. We had hoped that it would reverse the invisibility powder and return the creature to its normal size—but that's not what happened.

Oh, the creature was visible, all right . . . but only for a moment. Just long enough for us to see that it was changing again . . . and it was growing even *bigger!*

17

The creature in the garden became visible right before our very eyes. It was one of the iguanas, all right, but it was enormous.

And it wasn't entirely visible. It flashed on and off, on and off like a neon green light. For a second, I thought we might have hurt it.

Not so.

While the iguana flashed, it also began to change. It began to look less like an iguana, and more like a small dinosaur! It sprouted fangs that were long and sharp, and it's nose grew into a snout. The reptile didn't look like a cute iguana anymore . . . it looked like a terrible, vicious beast!

"Run!" Ryan shouted. It was the best idea I'd heard all day!

We both spun and sprang, running as fast as our legs could carry us. We darted around the hedges and across our yard, and we didn't stop until we were safely inside.

I slammed the front door behind me and locked it.

"Oh . . . man," Ryan heaved, trying to catch his breath. "We are in trouble now!"

I ran to the telephone and dialed the number of Goofy Stuff, Incorporated. Ryan ran to the window to see what the creature was doing.

"It's becoming invisible again!" he cried out. "It's . . . it's still gigantic . . . *but now it's invisible!*"

I held the phone to my ear. Thankfully, the line wasn't busy anymore. It rang a couple of times, then the man answered again. It was the same guy I talked to the first time.

"Please," I gasped. "You have to help us. We're in a lot of trouble."

"Calm down, calm down," the man said.

"You're talking so fast I can hardly understand you. Now . . . what's the problem?"

"We made an iguana invisible," I said.

"What?!?!?" the man gasped. "You're not supposed to use the invisibility powder on reptiles! It says so in the instructions!"

"My brother threw away the instructions," I explained frantically. "Anyway, we tried to make him visible again by putting baking soda on him, like you said."

"YOU TRIED TO REVERSE THE INVISIBILITY OF A REPTILE WITH BAKING SODA?!?!?!" he shouted.

"Is . . . is that bad?" I asked.

"Bad?!?!? *Bad?!?!? It's awful! It's the worst thing you could have done!!!"*

"Why?" I asked quickly. "What's going to happen?"

"First of all, the baking soda will indeed reverse the creature. For instance, if it was a nice creature before, it will become mean. If it ate plants before, then now it will eat meat. And it will grow even bigger than it was before. Bigger

. . . and *meaner*. And it probably won't look anything like an iguana."

"Alyssa?" I heard Ryan stammer from the window in the living room. "Alyssa . . . ?"

I turned my head to look at him. He was staring out the window. His eyes were wide, and he was trembling.

"There are huge footprints appearing in the grass," he said shakily. *"It's coming, Alyssa! It's coming for us!"*

18

"Quick!" I shouted to the man on the phone. "I need to know what to do!"

"Well, there's nothing you can do, except—"

"—there must be something! We have to stop this . . . this *thing!*"

"The only thing you can do is feed the creature cat food," he exclaimed. "It's the only way."

What?!?!? I thought. *Cat food?!?!? That's ridiculous! How would cat food turn the creature—whatever it had become—back into an ordinary, everyday, iguana?!?!*

"It's something in the way the cat food is made," he continued. "If you can get the creature to eat a can or two of cat food, it *might* return to its normal state."

"Iguanas won't eat cat food!" I said. "Besides . . . it's probably bad for them anyway!"

"If you used the invisibility powder on an iguana, it's not an iguana any longer, young lady. It's a dangerous creature. A *very* dangerous creature."

From the living room, Ryan spoke. "I can see huge footprints forming all over the yard!" he cried. "Whatever is making them is big . . . and invisible."

"What if it won't eat cat food?" I asked the man on the phone.

"Then I'm afraid there's nothing you can do," the man said. "Have a good day."

"Wait!" I cried. "I have another ques—"
Click.
The man had hung up.

"He's going around the tree in our yard!"

Ryan reported. "I can see where he's walking by the footprints forming in the yard!"

Suddenly, Ryan dived away from the window! He hit the floor, rolled, stood up, and ran past me.

"Run!" he shouted. *"He's attacking! The thing is attacking the house!"*

19

Now, you might think that what was happening was funny. But let me tell you . . . if you were in my shoes, you'd be terrified, just like I was. We had no idea what the creature wanted, or what it was capable of. The only thing we knew was that it was invisible, and it was huge. And it was part iguana, whatever it was.

I followed Ryan down the hall.

"Where are you going?!?!" I shrieked.

"The basement! We can hide in the basement, and lock the door if that thing gets in the house!"

Ryan bounded down the stairs with me right

behind him. He reached the basement door, flung it open, and darted in. I followed, turned, and slammed the door shut. I turned the lock and heard a heavy *thud*.

"Whew," I said. "We made it."

We backed away from the door and listened. At any moment, I expected to hear the sounds of shattering glass and crunching wood as the creature tried to get inside. Thankfully, we didn't hear anything except our own heaving breath.

"What did the guy on the phone say?" Ryan asked.

"He said that we have to feed the thing cat food," I replied.

"What?" he responded. "Why cat food?"

"He didn't say. The only thing he said was that there is something in the cat food that will reverse the invisibility powder, and turn the creature back to an iguana."

"That's crazy!" Ryan exclaimed.

"I know," I agreed. "But that's what he says."

"How are we going to get him to eat cat

food?" Ryan asked.

"You've got me," I answered. "Right now, I'm more concerned about him not eating *us!*"

We heard a noise from upstairs, but it sounded like it came from outside. We have a couple of windows in the basement, but they are near the ceiling.

Ryan walked to the window, but he wasn't tall enough to look outside.

"Help me with this table," he said, and I walked over to him. We have a large wood dining table in our basement that we don't use anymore. It's really heavy, but if we could move it over to the window, Ryan or I could climb on top of it and look outside.

We grabbed the table top and tried to lift it, but it was too heavy.

"Let's try and drag it over," I said, and instead of lifting, we pulled.

That worked. It was difficult, but we were able to scooch the table, inch by inch, over to the window. In doing so, Ryan knocked over a box filled with odds and ends. One of the things that fell out was an old pair of three-dimensional glasses. One lens was blue and the other was red, and they were used for watching 3-D movies. I had forgotten that I still had them.

Ryan picked up the 3-D glasses and put them on.

"What are you doing?" I asked.

"Well, you never know," he replied. "Maybe I'll be able to see that creature with these things."

"They're 3-D glasses, you goof! They won't let you see anything that's invisible!"

"Hey, you never know," Ryan replied, climbing on the table. He stood up, and looked out the window.

"Be careful," I said.

"You're not my mom."

"No, but I'm your older sister. I'm supposed to look after you. You said so yourself last night."

Ryan didn't say anything.

"What do you see?" I asked.

"Nothing. Everything looks pretty funky with these glasses on. I'll bet—*holy cow!*"

Ryan jumped so high he almost banged his

head on the ceiling!

"What!?!?!" I exclaimed. *"What do you see?!?"*

"Oh my gosh! There he is! I can see him plain as day!"

"What?!?!?" I cried. "What do you see!?!?" I leapt up onto the table and gazed out the window. I could see a picnic table and a tree in the back yard, along with our fence, but nothing else.

"He's right there!" Ryan pointed frantically. "I can see him! He's right there, by the picnic table!"

"Let me see your glasses!" I demanded, raising my hands up.

Ryan lowered the glasses. "Now he's gone!" He placed the glasses over his eyes again. "Now he's back! It's the glasses! *I can see him with the 3-D glasses!"*

"Let me see!" I pleaded again.

Ryan took the glasses off and handed them to me. "He's right over there," he pointed, "by the picnic table."

I put the 3-D glasses on and looked where

Ryan was pointing . . . and when I saw the creature, I screamed in terror.

20

What I saw in the yard was definitely *not* an iguana. I mean . . . it *might* have been an iguana at one time, but not anymore. What I was seeing looked more like some freaky lizard from a movie or a cartoon. He was the size of a small car, and he had dark brown scales and long, sharp claws that curled in. His eyes were like fire, and his nostrils flared as he breathed.

And *wings. The creature actually had wings!*

"Can you see it?" Ryan whispered, and for the first time, I noticed that he was shaking like a leaf on a tree.

"Y . . . yes," I stammered. "I . . . I can't believe it! Did you see its wings!?!?"

Ryan nodded. "Do you think it's real?" he asked.

"Of course it's real," I said. "Look at the footprints it's making in the grass." I lowered the glasses from my face. When I did, the creature disappeared. I could see footprints in the grass, but the creature had vanished. When I looked through the glasses again, the beast returned.

"This is just getting worse and worse," I said. "It was bad enough that we turned the iguanas invisible. Now we've created a monster!"

"Man, I can't wait to see the look on Stephen's face when he sees what his pet looks like now!" Ryan said.

"You think this is funny?!?!" I scolded.

"No, I don't. I think it's scary. How are we going to get that thing to eat cat food?"

I shook my head. "I don't know," I replied, "but the guy at he company said that it was the only way."

"That thing looks like it could eat a horse!"

I began to realize what kind of trouble we were in. And not just us, either . . . but the whole neighborhood. This awful creature was on the loose, and no one could see it.

But at least *we* could. As long as we had the 3-D glasses, we could see the creature. We would know where he was, so we could stay out of his way.

"What's he doing now?" Ryan asked.

"He's just standing there, looking around," I replied. "It doesn't look like he's doing much of anything . . . no, wait a minute—now he's moving."

"Where's he going?"

"I don't know. He just made a circle around the picnic table."

I watched as the enormous beast walked on all fours around the wood table. It was strange . . . in some ways, he still resembled an iguana. But in other ways, he looked like some creepy dragon.

"What's he doing now?" Ryan asked.

I watched as the creature slowly lowered itself to the grass.

"It looks like . . . it looks like he's going to go to sleep!" I said. "He's curled up on the ground, and he just put his head down. Now his eyes are closing!"

"Let me see!" Ryan said, snatching the glasses from my face. "Wow! You were right! I think he's taking a nap!"

"Which might give us time," I said.

"Time for what?" Ryan asked, still looking out through the window.

"A plan," I said. "A plan to get rid of this thing and change him back to an iguana."

Now Ryan removed the 3-D glasses from his eyes. He turned and looked at me.

"What's your plan?" he asked. When I explained my idea, his eyes lit up. "That just might work!" he exclaimed. "In fact, that sounds pretty easy!"

Well, it *sounded* easy.

But it wasn't going to be easy. We'd forgotten one important thing . . . there were *two* invisible iguanas, and not *one*.

Trouble was on its way . . . and *fast*.

21

My plan was this:

While the creature was sleeping, one of us would run to the store and buy some cat food. Somehow, we would have to try and feed it to the creature in the yard. I hadn't figured that part out yet.

"You go to the store," I said as we quietly made our way back up the stairs, "and I'll wait here and keep an eye on the creature in the yard."

Ryan shook his head. "Huh-uh," he said. "Other way around. I'm not going outside with that ugly lizard out there."

I didn't want to spend time arguing, so I told him that I would go.

"I'll go out the front door and run up to the grocery store," I said. "You keep an eye on the iguana — or whatever it is — that's in back. I'll be back as soon as I can.

"What if the creature sees you?" Ryan asked.

"He's sleeping," I said. "If I'm quiet, he won't notice me . . . I hope."

"I hope so, too," Ryan said. "If you get eaten by an invisible iguana, Mom and Dad are going to be pretty mad."

Which didn't make a lot of sense, but I ignored it.

"Let me see those glasses," I said. "I want to double-check once more to make sure the creature is still sleeping."

Ryan handed me his glasses and I tip-toed through the kitchen and looked out the window into the back yard. The strange beast was still asleep in the grass.

"Okay," I whispered, taking off the 3-D glasses and handing them to him. "I'm on my way. I'll go to the store, buy some cat food, and be back as quick as I can."

I strode to the front door.

"Wait!" Ryan said. "Take one of the walkie-talkies! That way, if the giant green thing wakes up, I can radio you and let you know!"

"Good idea," I said, nodding. Ryan and I got a walkie-talkie set for Christmas, and we use them a lot, especially when we go to the park or on our camping trips. They're a lot of fun . . . but today, they just might save my life!

Ryan retrieved the radios from his bedroom and handed me one. We checked them out to make sure the batteries weren't dead.

"Okay," I said. "All set. I'll be back in few minutes."

I opened the door slowly, being careful not to make any noise. Then I stepped out onto the porch.

"Hurry back," Ryan said.

"I will," I replied. I stepped off the porch and began running. I ran across the grass and turned onto the sidewalk . . . but I didn't get any farther.

Suddenly, I was sent sprawling into the air! I landed with a thud, and I winced in pain as my shoulder hit the hard cement. It was like I had tripped over a stump or something, but when I turned to see what had tripped me, there was nothing there!

I looked back at the house. Ryan was watching me from the window, and I saw him put on the 3-D glasses.

Then I saw his mouth open in an expression of shock. He raised the radio to his mouth, and then I heard his voice sputter from the radio in my pocket.

"It's the other iguana!" he cried. *"You tripped over him! He's two feet away from you right now . . . and he doesn't look happy!"*

22

I didn't move a muscle. My shoulder hurt from the fall and I wanted to rub it, but I didn't dare. I didn't think it was broken or anything, but boy . . . I sure hit the cement hard.

The radio sputtered again, and Ryan's voice continued. *"I don't think you have to worry,"* he said. *"It's the other iguana . . . but he doesn't look like the nasty one in the back yard."*

I sure was relieved to hear that! Then I suddenly remembered . . . we hadn't put baking soda on this iguana! Maybe it was tame, just like it had always been. Maybe the powder had only made the creature larger. And invisible, of course.

I carefully reached into my pocket and pulled out the two-way radio. I held it up to my mouth.

"How . . . how big is he?" I asked quietly.

"He's about as long as you are," Ryan replied.

"Is he coming after me?"

"Nope. He's just laying there on the cement."

"Okay," I said. *"Let me know if he moves."*

I stood up slowly, holding the radio in front of my mouth.

"He's not doing anything," Ryan reported. *"He's just watching you."*

I backed away slowly.

"He's still not doing anything," Ryan said. *"Actually, now he looks kind of bored."*

"I thought you said he looked angry," I replied.

"Yeah, he did . . . just after you stepped on him. Now, he looks like he's going to fall asleep, just like the other one."

Good. If *he* was going to sleep, then I still had a chance to get to the store. Maybe the cat food would work for *both* of the iguanas!

"Okay," I spoke into the radio. *"I'm on my*

way. I'll be right back."

"*I just looked in the back yard,*" Ryan replied. "*The other iguana . . . or whatever it is . . . is still asleep. Hurry back!*"

I spun and took off running again. I ran as fast as I could, and I only stopped when I reached the highway. No cars were coming, so I sprinted across the intersection and darted into the grocery store.

I hurried to the pet aisle . . . and now I had another problem. Which brand of cat food would work the best? Was there any difference? Should it be canned cat food, or cat food in a bag?

I decided to go with four cans of cat food, since it was cheaper. I hoped it wouldn't make any difference . . . and I hoped it would be enough.

"Looks like you've got a hungry kitty," the woman at the checkout counter said as she rang up the cat food.

"Uh, yeah, I guess you could say that," I replied.

She put the four cans in a bag and I quickly

left the store. At the street corner, I waited for a few cars to go by. Then I dashed madly back across the intersection, swinging the grocery bag in my hand and clutching the radio in the other. When I reached the other side of the street, I placed the radio in front of my mouth.

"Got it!" I exclaimed. Seconds later, the radio crackled. Ryan's voice came through loud and clear.

"Both of the creatures are still sleeping," he said. "I think it's going to work!"

"I'll be home in a minute," I said. "Don't do anything to scare them off!"

I ran down the sidewalk, block after block, until our house came into view. Then I slowed down and spoke into the radio again.

"Is the one in the front still there?" I asked.

"Yes," Ryan replied over the radio. "I think it's still sleeping."

"We'll try that one first," I said.

All of a sudden, I realized a problem that I hadn't thought of:

I didn't have a can opener!

"Ryan!" I said into the radio. "Can you bring me a can opener?"

"A what?" he replied.

"A can opener! I can't open the cat food without a can opener!"

I saw Ryan disappear from the window, and then return a moment later. "Got one," his voice boomed from the radio.

"I'll come to the porch and get it," I said, walking across the lawn toward the house.

He opened the door and stepped out onto the porch. He sure looked silly with those 3-D glasses on!

I took the can opener from him and opened a can of cat food.

"Let me have the 3-D glasses," I said, "so I can see where the iguana is."

Ryan removed the glasses from his face and handed them to me. I put them on and turned.

"Wow," I whispered when I saw the giant iguana sleeping on the sidewalk. It really *did* look like a regular iguana . . . except it was ten times its normal size!

"Uh-oh," Ryan said. "We've got trouble."

"How?" I asked . . . but Ryan didn't have to answer. Down the block, a kid was riding his bicycle on the sidewalk. *Fast.*

"He's headed right for the iguana!" I exclaimed.

Ryan waved his hands and shouted. "Hey! You! Look out!"

The kid on the bike was really moving. He saw Ryan, but he just kept pedaling like crazy.

"He can't look out," I told Ryan. "He can't see the iguana!"

I thought about running across the lawn to divert him away from the giant reptile . . . but it was already too late. As we watched, the kid, still pedaling furiously, ran his bike straight into the sleeping iguana!

23

Wham!

The kid didn't have a chance. There was no way he could see the giant iguana in front of him, and he hit the creature at full speed.

His bike stopped instantly, like it had hit an invisible brick wall. The kid went flying forward, over the handlebars and into the air.

"Aaaaaaaaggggghhhhh!!" he screamed. Then he hit the ground, tumbling over and rolling into the grass.

The iguana was equally dazed. Through the 3-D glasses, I watched as it got up on its feet and looked around.

"What . . . what happened?!?!" the kid stammered, shaking his head. "What did I hit?!?!"

"An iguana! Ryan shouted, running up to him. "A giant invisible iguana!"

The kid looked at Ryan like he was from outer space. "You're crazy," he said.

"No, really!" Ryan exclaimed. "He's right over there, I think. I'm not sure, though, because I don't have the 3-D glasses on." Ryan looked at me. Of course, I could still see the iguana, but Ryan and the other kid couldn't.

"He's right," I said to the kid. "It's right there. Right by your bike. Here." I removed the 3-D glasses and held them out for the kid. "See for yourself," I said.

"Get away from me!" the kid shrieked. "You guys are freaks!"

"No, really," Ryan said. "Take a look."

"I'm getting away from you two kooks," he said, and he leapt to his feet. "You guys are weird."

He ran to pick up his bicycle . . . but he didn't get far.

"Look out!" I screamed.

Too late.

The kid ran right into the iguana, and for the second time, he was sent flying. He tumbled into the grass, rolled a couple times, then stopped.

"What did you do that for?!?!" he demanded angrily.

"We didn't do anything," I said. "You ran into the invisible iguana!"

"Yeah, well now you're in for it! Both of you!" The kid leapt to his feet and doubled his hands into fists. "If it's a fight you want, that's what you'll get," he said.

Ryan shook his head and backed away. "No! No! We don't want to fight," he explained frantically. "There really *is* an invisible iguana right by you!"

"We're not kidding," I pleaded. "Honest! We didn't knock you off your bike . . . and we didn't trip you. Here." Again, I held out the glasses for the kid to put on. I knew that if he saw the iguana for himself, he would believe us.

But he wasn't about to take them. He clenched his fists tightly, ready to take us both on.

Whether the kid was actually going to fight or not, we'll never know. Because the giant invisible iguana had had enough. It reared back, opened its mouth . . . *and attacked the kid right where he was standing!*

24

The kid charged for us . . . but the iguana opened up its huge jaws and lunged forward, catching a piece of the boy's shirt. This stopped the kid altogether, and he tried to turn to see what had stopped him.

"Hey!" he shouted as he spun. When he turned and didn't see anything, but realized that *something* was holding onto him, he freaked.

"*Aaaaaaahhhh!!!*" he cried. "*Something's got me! Something has hold of me!!*"

"*I told you!*" I exclaimed. "*It's an invisible iguana! He's huge!*"

This did nothing but freak the kid out even more. He struggled to get away, but through the 3-D glasses I could see that the iguana wasn't about to let go. He was chewing on the kid's shirt, and I really began to get scared. Ordinary iguanas wouldn't do something like this . . . but what if this one really *did* hurt the boy? What could we do to stop it, if anything?

The kid was really flailing now, and the iguana's jaws were still clamped around part of his loose shirt, tighter than ever.

Suddenly, there was a loud tearing sound, and the shirt gave way. The kid lost his balance and fell to the ground, but he wasted no time in jumping to his feet and snatching up his bicycle. He leapt onto the seat and his feet immediately began pumping the pedals. In seconds, he was already at the next block.

"Freaks!" he shouted, as he gave Ryan and me a glance over his shoulder. *"You guys are nothing but freaks!"*

Ryan and I didn't pay any attention to his comment. I think we were both just glad that the kid hadn't been hurt. That had been a close one.

And speaking of close ones, the giant iguana was still on the sidewalk . . . only now, he was munching on part of the shirt that had ripped!

"Let me see!" Ryan said, snapping the 3-D glasses from my face.

"I think he's hungry!" I exclaimed. "Let's try and feed him the cat food!"

While Ryan watched the creature through the 3-D glasses, I hastily opened a can of cat food.

"I need the glasses to see where he is!" I said. "Unless *you* want to try and feed him."

Ryan removed the glasses from his face and handed them to me. "Give it a whirl," he said.

"Chicken," I snarled. He just shrugged.

I put the glasses on, and the iguana came into view. He still had a small piece of the boy's shirt dangling from the side of his jaw. The giant reptile was looking right at me.

I wondered how close I would need to get. Would I have to get right up to the creature? And if I did, would he try and attack me, too? What if he decided that I tasted better than the cat food?

Maybe he wouldn't like the cat food, anyway, and would go after me and Ryan.

"What are you waiting for?" my brother asked.

I didn't answer him. Instead, I took a step toward the giant, green beast.

It turned its head and stared at me.

I took another step toward it, and the iguana opened its mouth. The remaining piece of the shirt fell from its jaw and landed on the sidewalk.

"What's he doing?" Ryan asked quietly.

"Nothing, really," I replied. "He's just looking at me."

Slowly . . . *very, very slowly* . . . I bent down, holding the can of cat food as far out as I could. I wondered if the beast could smell it.

My plan was to place the can of cat food onto the sidewalk, then back up slowly and see what the iguana would do.

I didn't have a chance. Without warning, the giant creature reared up. Its mouth was open, and its eyes burned with fury. I tried to run, but it was impossible . . . because the iguana had already sprung! Suddenly, I was forced to the grass as the enormous reptile came down upon me!

25

I tried to roll away, but the creature's claw came down on my shoulder, pinning me to the grass. The can of cat food fell from my hand and hit the sidewalk with a clang. I have never been so scared in my entire life! There was no way I could get away if I tried!

"*Ryan!*" I shrieked. "*Help me!*"

"I can't see him!" Ryan yelled.

"*He's . . . he's on top of me! He's going to –* "

Suddenly, the creature backed away! He raised his claw from my shoulder, and I was no longer pinned to the grass beneath his weight. I seized the opportunity and rolled sideways, away from the iguana. I almost lost the 3-D glasses, but I caught them before they slid down my nose.

I took a few steps and stood next to my brother in the grass. He was panicking.

"I would have helped you," he began, "but I couldn't see the iguana! I didn't know what he was doing!"

I watched the giant reptile as it slowly sniffed the open can of cat food.

"What's he doing?" Ryan asked.

"Shhh!" I whispered. *"He's sniffing the cat food!"*

I watched as the iguana continued sniffing around the can. Then he drew back and looked at it. With one of his claws, he reached down and toyed with the can. A small clump of cat food spilled onto the cement, and the iguana leaned down and sniffed it again. Then he opened his mouth and ate the tiny morsel.

"I think he likes it!" I said. *"He's eating some of it!"*

The iguana then knocked the can around

some more, until more cat food spilled out. Then it lowered its head and gobbled up the spilled contents.

"He's eating it," I reported to Ryan. *"He's really eating it! He seems to like it!"*

"Yeah," Ryan replied quietly. *"But is it changing him back into a normal-sized iguana?"*

"Not yet," I said. *"He's still . . . wait a minute! Something's happening!"*

The iguana suddenly got a puzzled look on its face, like it was wondering what was going on. Then it began to move and twist. It was really freaky, watching it . . . and it began to shrink! The creature was getting smaller!

"Hey!" Ryan exclaimed. *"I think I just saw something!"*

I removed my glasses. Ryan was right! Without the 3-D glasses I didn't think I would be able to see the iguana . . . but now I could see strange flashes of green!

"He's becoming visible again!" I cried happily. *"It's working! It's really working!"*

In a few more seconds, the iguana was back to

its original size . . . and it was completely visible! It just sat on the sidewalk in the sun, acting as if nothing had ever happened.

"He's back to normal!" Ryan cried out. "He's a regular iguana again!"

I walked over to where the iguana sat, and carefully picked it up.

"How are you, buddy?" I asked the creature.

"Is that Jack or Jill?" Ryan asked.

I shook my head. "I can't tell them apart. Stephen probably can, though."

"Let's hope it works on the one in the backyard," Ryan said.

Jeepers! I nearly forgot!

"Let's go!" I said. We walked quickly across the yard and into the house.

"Let me have those glasses," Ryan said. I handed them to him.

"I'm going to put him back in his cage," I said. "I'll be right there."

I carried the iguana into Ryan's bedroom and placed him gently into the cage. Then I went to find Ryan. I really was hoping that the strange beast in the backyard would eat the cat food.

Ryan was standing by the back door, and his mouth was open in shock.

"What's the matter?" I asked. Ryan took off the 3-D glasses and looked at me. He was horrified.

"The creature!" he exclaimed. *"It's . . .it's gone!"*

26

I held the 3-D glasses up to my eyes and searched the yard.

No creature.

"It couldn't have gone far," I said. "We were in the front yard for just a few minutes."

I looked up into the sky . . . and I didn't like what I saw. I gasped.

"What?" Ryan asked. "What is it?!?"

I pointed up into the sky. "It . . . it can *fly!*"

It was true. The creature was using its huge wings, and it was flying in the sky like some prehistoric bird!

"What?!?!?" Ryan said. "Let me see!" He held out his hands, and I gave him the 3-D glasses. He placed them over his eyes and searched the sky.

"I see him!" he shouted. "He really can fly!"

All of a sudden, I realized how strange this whole day had become. What was happening was so crazy that there was no one that would believe us! We tried to call for help, but everyone thought that we were nuts.

I guess I couldn't blame them, though. I wasn't sure that *I* believed what was going on.

"Now what do we do?" Ryan asked.

"We have to follow it!" I said. "There's no telling what it might do or where it might go!"

"But what if it flies for hundreds of miles?" Ryan asked. "What then?"

"We follow it," I said. "We have to follow that thing and try and turn it back into a regular iguana. Where is it now?"

Ryan pointed. "Up there. He's not flying very fast. Actually, he looks like he's circling."

"What's he circling?"

"I can't tell," Ryan said. "But it looks like he's probably over the park."

"Let's go," I said. "Don't let him out of your sight."

"That might be kind of hard," Ryan said, "because now it looks like he's going to land."

"Come on!" I said, and I ran to the front of the house. "Let's get on our bikes!"

I pushed open the front door, ran across the porch, and darted into the garage. I put the cans of unopened cat food and the can opener in my bike basket. Ryan was right behind me, and both of us grabbed our bikes and tore out the driveway.

"He's got to be in the park!" Ryan shouted. "I think that's where he landed!"

And it was then that we heard it. Horns honking, people screaming . . . and a loud *crash*.

Something awful had happened.

27

The noise made me pedal even faster, and my mind raced. *What had happened?* I wondered. *Was anyone hurt? Had the creature attacked someone?*

We raced around the block, our bikes flying down the sidewalk. Finally, the park came into view. I could see a few cars and some people gathered around

"Up ahead!" I shouted. "There's something going on at the entrance of the park!"

And there was, that was for sure. The closer we got, the more I realized that something serious had happened.

"What is it, can you tell?" Ryan asked from behind me.

"Not yet," I said. "Come on!"

Soon, more cars were visible. Most of them were parked in a parking lot, but there were a few parked out by the road.

And an ice cream truck. There was a colorful ice cream truck parked off to the side of the parking lot. Lots of people were standing around.

"Uh-oh," Ryan said. "I hope the creature didn't cause an accident."

"It might be a lot worse than that," I said.

We approached the ice cream truck, and I heard a man speaking.

"It's okay, folks, just a small accident. Nobody hurt, just a lot of ice cream spilled."

I hopped off my bike and began to push it closer to the truck, and Ryan did the same. We had to weave in and out among a lot of people that had gathered. Finally, we were right up next to the ice cream truck . . . and it was a mess!

"No problem, folks," the man was saying. "Just spilled a few tubs of ice cream. Nobody hurt."

"Look at all that spilled ice cream!" Ryan hissed. *"It's everywhere!"*

And it was. It looked like some tubs of ice cream had fallen from the back of the truck. They had exploded open on the road, and ice cream was everywhere! It had already started to melt on the hot pavement. Several cars had to slam on their brakes to keep from sliding into the goo.

But thankfully, no one had been hurt.

The man that had been talking walked right in front of us, carrying a broken tub of ice cream.

"How did it happen?" I asked him.

He stopped. "You know . . . it was the strangest thing. I was driving along, and all of a sudden, I felt a loud thump on the back of my truck. Heavy, too. For a minute, I thought something had fallen from the sky."

Ryan and I looked at each other, our eyes wide in terror.

"Then," the man continued, "tubs of ice cream began to fall from the truck. I don't know how it happened, because I always make sure that they're secured." He scratched his head. "Sure made a terrible mess, that's for sure."

People had finally started to drive off, and the bystanders that had been gathered around were now leaving. There was ice cream all over the street and even past the curb and into the grass.

"Would you like some help cleaning up?" I asked.

"Well, that's nice of you . . . but I think I can handle it. Sure is a shame to waste all of that ice cream," he said.

"I . . . I don't . . . don't think it's going to waste," Ryan stammered. He sounded nervous, and I looked at him. He had on the 3-D glasses and was staring at the other side of the street where the entrance to the park was.

"Alyssa!" he hissed in my ear. *"The creature! It's on the other side of the street . . . eating the spilled ice cream!"*

28

I looked in the direction that Ryan was looking, but, of course, I couldn't see anything.

However . . . .

I watched closely . . . *and I could see clumps of ice cream disappearing!* Talk about freaky!

The good news was that no one else seemed to notice it. There were still a few people around, but no one seemed to see the blobs of ice cream that were simply vanishing into thin air.

Or, the ice cream *seemed* to be vanishing, anyway . . . but I knew better.

"Let me see," I said. Ryan handed me the 3-D

glasses and I put them on.

"Wow!" I said. *"He's really gobbling that stuff up!"*

"Who's gobbling up what?" the man asked.

Gulp! He heard me talking!

"Uh . . . ummm . . . what I meant was . . . ."

I suddenly realized that if someone else saw the invisible creature, they would have to believe us. Maybe if the ice cream man saw the invisible iguana with wings, maybe he would help us out.

"Right over there," I said, handing the man my 3-D glasses.

"Over where," he said. "What do I do with these?"

"Just put them on and tell me what you see," I said. My hope grew. I knew that he would see the creature . . . and then he might help us. We could explain everything to him.

This whole thing might have a happy ending, after all.

The man put the glasses on. "Boy, these sure make everything look weird," he said.

"Look over there," I said, pointing toward the

entrance of the park.

"Over . . . *OH MY GOSH!!!*" He pulled the glasses away from his face, and his eyes were popping right out of his head. He raised the glasses again and gasped.

Suddenly, the man lurched to the side . . . and fell over into the grass! *The ice cream man had fainted!*

29

Ryan and I knelt down to help the fallen man. His eyes were closed, and he was on his back in the grass. The 3-D glasses had fallen from his face and landed next to him. I quickly picked them up and shoved them into my pocket.

"What happened?" Ryan asked.

"I think he fainted when he saw the creature!" I exclaimed frantically.

"What do we do?!?!" he asked. We were both a little freaked out. "Do you think he's hurt?"

Suddenly, the man opened his eyes. He blinked and glanced around nervously, like he was unsure of where he was.

"Wha . . . what happened?" he stammered, propping himself up on his elbows.

"You fainted," I said, and I was just about to explain to him why when he leaned forward and got to his feet.

"Must be the heat," he said, shaking his head. "It sure is a hot one today. I'm going to have to be careful."

"Are you sure you're all right?" I asked.

"Yeah," the man said. I think I'm—"

He stopped speaking, suddenly noticing the spilled ice cream on the other side of the street. He paused and squinted, like he was in deep concentration. Then he shook his head and laughed.

"Must have been the heat," he said. "I guess I'm just going to have to get out of the sun."

I looked at Ryan, and he looked back at me and shrugged.

"Are you sure you don't need any help cleaning up the ice cream?" I asked.

The man shook his head. "No, but thank you.

Most of it is melted anyway. I think I'm going to go home early and rest. The heat has really gotten to me today. You know . . . for a moment, I thought I saw a giant green lizard with wings on the other side of the street, eating ice cream."

"Imagine that," Ryan said, raising his eyebrows.

"You kids have a good day, and thanks for offering to help."

"No problem," I said. The man hopped into his truck and slowly drove off. He honked once and waved out the window. Ryan and I waved back.

As soon as he was gone, I pulled the 3-D glasses out of my pocket and put them on.

It was just as I thought—the creature was gone.

"Do you see him?" Ryan asked.

"No," I said, shaking my head and scanning the park. "No . . . wait! There he is! Over by the fountain!"

We picked up our bikes and pushed them across the street and entered the park.

"Let me see," Ryan said, and he snatched the glasses from my face. He stopped to put them on.

"He's right over there by the water fountain," I said, pointing. Ryan looked in the direction of where my arm extended. His jaw fell.

"Not anymore!" he cried. *"He's over there by the hot dog stand . . . and there are people all around him!"*

30

I snatched the glasses from my brother and held them up to my eyes. Sure enough, the strange iguana-like creature was only a few feet from a bunch of people! Of course, no one could see the beast, but that was a problem, too. They might walk into him and fall flat on their face!

But what would happen if the creature attacked one of the people? It would be awful, especially since no one could see the creature. No one would know where to run or how to get away!

"What's it doing?" Ryan asked.

"Nothing, at the moment," I replied.

"We have to do something, quick."

"Yeah . . . but what?" I answered. "There's nothing we can do at the moment."

"Well, we have to lure the creature away from all of those people," Ryan said.

I watched the creature as it sniffed the air.

"I think it's picking up a whiff of someone's hot dog," I said.

"That's it!" Ryan said. "Do you have any money left?"

"Only a dollar," I replied.

Ryan looked over at the hot dog stand. "That's enough for two hot dogs," he said. "Give me your dollar. I'll buy two hot dogs, and maybe we can lure the creature away from the crowd of people."

"Then we can feed him the cat food!" I exclaimed. "It might work!"

I gave Ryan my dollar and he ran up to the hot dog stand. Fortunately, there weren't many people in line. While he waited, I kept the 3-D glasses on so I could see the invisible creature. Some people looked at me strangely, but I didn't care. I had other things to worry about.

It took Ryan less than a minute to buy two hot dogs. He handed one to me, and we got ready.

"Hang on a second," I said. "I'm going to open a can of cat food so we're ready."

I opened up the can and left it in my bicycle basket.

"Just how are we going to do this?" Ryan asked.

"One of us will place half of a hot dog on the ground in front of the creature," I explained, "and then we'll place another half hot dog a couple feet away. Then another, and another. Then, we'll put down the cat food."

"Kind of like leading him with bits of food, huh?" Ryan asked.

I nodded. "We have to entice the creature away from people before he eats the cat food," I said.

"And before he eats anyone," Ryan added. "Is he still nearby?"

"Right there," I said. "He looks like he's about ready to swipe someone's food. I think he's hungry."

"Good," Ryan said. "Let's get to work."

Since I had the glasses, I would place the first bit of food near the creature. I was a bit leery of getting too close to the beast, but so far it didn't seem like it was going to harm anyone. It seemed more interested in the hot dogs.

I tore one of the hot dogs in half.

"Here goes nothing," I said, and I walked slowly toward the creature, my arm stretched out, holding half of the hot dog.

When I was a few feet from the creature, I placed the hot dog on the ground. Then I stepped back and placed the other half on the ground.

Ryan stepped forward, and I pointed, indicating where he should put one half of his hot dog. Then he stepped back and placed the other one on the ground.

"It's working!" I whispered excitedly. *"The creature smells the first hot dog!"*

Through the 3-D glasses, I watched as the

large reptile crept up to the hot dog and ate it with a single gulp. It then wasted no time finding the next one, and the one after that.

"Let me see!" Ryan said, and I handed him the glasses.

"That's cool!" he whispered.

I snapped up the open can of cat food that I had placed in my bicycle basket.

"Let me have those glasses back, so I can see where to put the cat food," I said.

"Be careful," Ryan said.

"You're the one who should be doing this," I said. "You're the one who got us into this mess."

"Hey, it's not my fault," he said.

I circled around a small group of people. So far, we had been able to draw the invisible beast away from the group, and keep them out of danger. Right now, the creature was gobbling up the remaining halves of the hot dogs.

To make it easy for the iguana to eat, I dumped the contents from the cat food can into the grass. That way, it wouldn't have to fumble around with the can itself.

Besides, I thought. *The thing might want to eat the can along with the food.*

I walked away from the pile of cat food in the grass. The invisible iguana was just finishing up the last hot dog, and I quickly walked up to Ryan's side.

"Where is he?" he asked.

I pointed. "Right over there, just as we'd hoped," I replied.

The creature stopped eating and sniffed the air. He turned his head, sniffed, and began to move.

"He's headed for the cat food!" I said. "It's going to work!"

A wave of relief went through my body. Everything was going to work out fine, after all. The creature was about to eat the cat food, and it would soon be just a regular iguana again.

And then . . . disaster struck.

31

From out of nowhere, a dog suddenly appeared. It probably belonged to someone in the park, because it had a collar and a leash . . . except no one was holding onto the leash! It ran right up to the pile of cat food in the grass . . . *and began eating it!*

"*Oh no!*" I cried. "*That silly dog is eating the cat food! He's going to wreck everything!*"

And the invisible iguana was *not* happy about it, either. At first, it just stopped and watched the dog gobble up the cat food. But then, it reared back and opened its mouth, like it was getting ready to attack the dog!

And here's the weird part: it looked like the dog could see the creature! It seemed to be looking at the beast while it chomped down the cat food.

Suddenly, the creature lunged for the dog. By now, the dog had finished up the cat food, but when the iguana attacked, he began barking and growling, running in circles around the giant reptile.

And people began to notice.

"What's that crazy dog doing over there?" someone asked. "He's barking and growling at nothing."

I lowered the 3-D glasses for a moment. Sure enough, that's what it looked like. It looked like the dog was running around in a circle, snapping and snarling at something that wasn't there.

Of course, Ryan and I knew better. So did the dog, for that matter.

The dog continued to circle the creature, and the invisible iguana was getting angrier and angrier. I knew that it was only a matter of moments before the enormous reptile would simply lash out at the dog with its powerful jaws and sharp teeth.

"Goober!" I heard someone shout. I turned to see a woman rushing toward the dog. *"Goober! You behave! Come here this instant!"*

"Uh-oh," Ryan said. *"I hope she doesn't get too close."*

The dog stopped its barking and turned to look at the woman . . . and it was the break that the creature needed. In one quick motion it spread its wings and rose up into the sky! The dog gave one more quick bark as if to warn the creature not to come back. Then, its owner was there, picking up the leash.

"Goober, you bad dog! I told you not to go anywhere!" The woman and the dog strode away.

"What just happened?" Ryan asked. I had forgotten that he couldn't see the creature without the glasses.

"The iguana is flying again!" I said, pointing up into the sky. *"It's up above the trees! Come on!"*

155

I'll tell you . . . I was getting really tired of this. Chasing an invisible beast around Springfield was not my ideal way of spending a day.

But now we had another problem. The iguana had once again taken flight. It was flying above the trees . . . and headed right for the heart of the city.

32

For the second time that day, we found ourselves following an invisible flying creature. Ryan and I wasted no time hopping back on our bikes and setting off after the strange reptile.

"Can you still see him?" Ryan asked every few seconds.

"Yes," I replied.

"Where's he heading?"

"I can't tell just yet," I said, "but at least he's not flying way up in the sky."

Truthfully, following him wasn't that hard. I

had to be careful to watch where I was going with the bike, but it was easy enough to glance up into the blue sky and see the weird creature flapping its gigantic wings.

We wound our bikes all around, past buildings and subdivisions, past the old state capital and the Illinois State Museum. For a minute, I thought that the iguana was going to land in the Adams Wildlife Sanctuary, which is a big nature preserve. It's huge, with tons of trees and hiking trails. If the iguana landed somewhere in there, we'd never find it!

Thankfully, the creature kept flying. It flew low, just above the trees, and it would sometimes hover in a particular spot for a second or two, and then continue on its way.

"Man . . . how long is that thing going to stay up there?" Ryan asked.

"I have no idea," I said. "The only thing I know is that we have to follow it. I have two cans of cat food left. I hope that's enough."

We wound around the city, following the strange, invisible beast. I thought that it was really wild that no one else could see this creature but us . . . and only when we were wearing the 3-D glasses.

Finally, after what seemed like hours of pedaling, the creature began to sink lower in the sky.

"I think he's coming down!" I shouted to Ryan. "I think he's landing!"

"Can you see where?" Ryan asked.

"No, there are too many trees in the way!"

We rounded a corner onto Seventh Street, and I immediately brought my bike to a screeching halt. Ryan was so close behind me that he almost crashed into me, and, in fact, had to turn his bike to miss me.

"Hey!" he exclaimed as he stopped his bike. "Watch what you're doing!"

I didn't answer him. I was looking through the 3-D glasses, watching the iguana, which had just landed.

"Where is he?" Ryan asked.

I didn't answer him. The only thing I could do was hand him the 3-D glasses so he could see for himself.

He took them from me and looked around.

"Holy cow!" he exclaimed. *"The thing landed on the roof of Abraham Lincoln's old home!"*

33

Now, here's one thing you need to know about Abraham Lincoln's home: there are *tons* of people around it all day. The house is now a museum, and lots of people come from all over to see Lincoln's boyhood home.

And a giant, iguana-like creature was now sitting on the roof!

"Come on!" I said to Ryan. "We've got to act fast!" I leapt off my bike and scooped up the last two cans of cat food and the can opener.

"What are we going to do!?!?" Ryan asked. "We can't go on the roof of Abraham Lincoln's house!"

"We'll have to wait for him to come down, or we can try and coax him down," I said. "Let me see those 3-D glasses."

Ryan had propped his bike up against a tree. He removed the glasses from his face and handed them to me. I put them on and looked up at the old building before us.

There were a few people coming out the front door, and a few were standing around the house, taking pictures. Abraham Lincoln's home is a popular tourist attraction in Springfield.

"How do you think we can coax him down?" Ryan asked.

"Maybe we won't have to!" I exclaimed excitedly. "Maybe we can feed the cat food to him on the roof!"

"What?!?!" Ryan exclaimed. "That's crazy. Even if we *could* do it, and he *did* change back into an iguana, he'd still be on the roof."

Ryan had a good point. We would have to wait for the beast to come down before we could try and feed it the cat food.

And so we sat down in the grass and waited. And waited. We waited for hours and hours. All the while, the creature sat on the roof, once in a while stretching or turning its head to look around.

Finally, late in the afternoon, we got a break. There was still a bunch of people around, milling about here and there, when all of sudden the creature on the roof spread its wings.

"Uh-oh," I said to Ryan. "Looks like something is happening."

I was afraid for a moment that the creature might climb up into the sky. Then we'd be off again, chasing the invisible flying reptile around the city of Springfield.

Thankfully, that's not what it did. It flapped its wings several times, circled the home, and landed in the grass near the sidewalk.

Perfect!

And another good thing: there wasn't anyone close by. Oh, there were a few people still going in and out of the home, but no one was near the invisible creature in the grass.

"This might be our only chance!" I said to Ryan. "Hand me the can opener!"

Ryan handed me the can opener and I went to work. It only took a few seconds to open both cans.

"Stay here," I said, leaping to my feet. "I'll put the cat food down as close as I can."

I hurried across the grass and along the sidewalk. The creature was facing the other way, so he hadn't spotted me . . . yet.

As I drew near, I could see just how ugly he really was. Iguanas are really kind of cute, but what this iguana had turned into wasn't so cute at all. And there was no way that I'd want one of these for a pet!

My plan was this: I would sneak up behind the beast as quietly as I could, and place the cat food in the grass. Then I would walk away. Hopefully, the creature would smell the food, then eat it.

I was only a few feet away now. I turned and shot a nervous glance toward my brother, who gave me the 'thumbs up' sign.

Yeah. Easy for him. He can't even see the creature without the glasses, and I'm the one doing the dirty work.

I turned back around and took another step. One more stride and I would be close enough to set the cat food on the ground. It was all going perfectly . . . until the creature discovered that I was there.

In a flash he had turned and confronted me. He reared back on his hind legs, and I have never been so afraid of anything in my entire life. The beast was tall . . . much taller than I was. His wings were spread and his mouth was open.

I froze. I mean . . . I couldn't have moved if I tried.

Which wasn't a good thing . . . because the creature slowly came at me, mouth open and teeth bared. His huge, softball-sized eyes burned into mine.

Closer and closer he came, until his jaws were only inches from my face. His nostrils flared. His breath smelled horrible, too, like he'd eaten a bunch of rotten onions.

But that wasn't the worst part. The worst part was when he leaned even closer, and opened his mouth even wider. I knew then that it was all over.

34

"What's wrong?" I heard Ryan say. But I couldn't answer him. I was about to be devoured by a giant, invisible reptile with stinky breath . . . and there wasn't anything I could do.

"What's wrong?" I heard Ryan ask again, only this time, his voice sounded closer.

Suddenly, the creature looked away, like he was staring behind me, over my shoulder.

It was the chance I needed.

With one swift move, I reached my fingers into the can of cat food and scooped out a handful. It was all wet and gooey, but I didn't mind. I reached up, threw the food into the open mouth of the beast . . . and ran. I turned and ran so fast that I think my sneakers left skid marks on the sidewalk!

"Hey!" Ryan shouted. He had been walking toward me . . . but when he saw me turn and bolt, he spun and ran himself.

"What's happening?!?!" he cried out. "What's going on!?!?"

"Just keep running!" I huffed.

We sprinted across the grass and didn't stop until we reached our bikes. I collapsed in a heap near a tree, and Ryan fell down next to me. Then we both turned to see what was happening to the iguana.

"What did you do?" he asked.

"I threw a handful of cat food into his mouth," I replied.

"You were that close to him?!?!" he asked.

I nodded. "It was scary. Really, really scary."

"I hope it works," he said.

I could see the creature through the 3-D glasses. He was chewing a little bit, but nothing

168

was happening.

All of a sudden, the reptile got a real strange look in its eye. It began twisting and turning and jumping up and down!

"I think it's working!" I said excitedly. "I think that he's changing!"

But now we had still *another* problem.

A woman had emerged from the Lincoln home. She was carrying her purse and a paper bag, walking along the sidewalk . . . *right toward the creature!*

Would she notice? Was the creature changing fast enough so that she would see it become visible again?

Suddenly, she stopped.

She stared.

She'd spotted the creature!

35

The woman dropped her purse and her bag. Her hands flew up to her face, and she covered her open mouth. She looked terrified!

On the sidewalk, the creature continued its bizarre transformation. It began to screech and scream, and then it began flashing. I no longer needed my 3-D glasses to see it.

And the woman on the sidewalk freaked out. She started screaming and yelling, and carrying on like crazy. The creature was still very big, but now it was visible, and Ryan and I could see it clearly.

Then, the woman ran screaming back into Abraham Lincoln's home.

"It's a monster!" she shrieked. *"A horrible, awful monster! It's after me! Agggghhhhhh!"*

She vanished into the home, screaming at the top of her lungs.

"It's shrinking, Alyssa!" Ryan exclaimed. "The creature is getting smaller!"

I can't tell you how relieved I was as I watched the giant creature shrink. In a few seconds, it was back to being a normal iguana again.

"Come on!" I said. "Let's go get him and take him home!"

But before we even started off, the terrified woman had returned from Lincoln's house, followed by a bunch of people.

"Awful!" she was saying. *"It's huge! With giant teeth and enormous eyes and —"*

She stopped speaking in mid-sentence. One of the men that had followed her out put his hands on his hips, and gestured toward the harmless iguana, soaking up the sun on the pavement.

"This," he began, "is the terrible beast?"

"Why, it's not even two feet long," said someone else. There were some chuckles of laughter, and the group began to walk back into the house.

"But . . . but . . . ." the woman stammered in cofusion. "It was gigantic! Really, it was!"

"Yeah, sure," someone said. Finally, the only person left standing on the sidewalk was the woman. I kind of felt bad that no one believed her. But I sure was glad that she wasn't hurt!

Ryan and I walked up to the iguana on the sidewalk.

"He's my pet," I explained, and I knelt down and gently picked up the creature in my arms.

"I could have sworn . . . ." the woman said, not finishing her sentence.

"What?" Ryan said.

The woman shrugged. "Oh, nothing." She smiled. "It was just my mind playing tricks on me," she said. "It was silly."

"Well, have a nice day," I said, and Ryan and

I walked back to our bikes. I placed the iguana in my bike basket, and we rode back home.

When we got back to our house, the first thing I did was check on Iggy. I was afraid that when I got home, he would be invisible, too . . . but he wasn't. What a relief.

Mom and Dad still weren't home yet, which was a good thing. My room was a mess, and so was Ryan's. We were able to get things cleaned up before they came home.

All during dinner, I thought about the strange things that had happened. I was going to tell Mom and Dad, but I knew they wouldn't believe me. I guess it was just going to be a secret between Ryan and me.

And Stephen. When Stephen came home and stopped by to pick up Jack and Jill, we would tell him. Maybe he would believe us, maybe he wouldn't. We'd have to wait and see.

- - - -

When Stephen returned the following week, he

was happy to see Jack and Jill. Even the two iguanas seemed happy to see their owner. Ryan and I were just glad that things ended up the way that they did.

And when we told him what happened, he believed us! He really did!

"All of this happened in one day?" he asked. He was standing in our living room, holding the cage that held the two iguanas.

"That's right," I said.

"Do you have any more of that invisibility powder?" he asked Ryan.

"No, but I ordered some more," he said. "But this time, I'm going to read the directions so we don't get into trouble like we did with your two iguanas. I know it sounds crazy, but every word of what we told you is true."

"Oh, I believe it," Stephen said. "That's the second creepiest story I've heard this week."

"Second?" I asked. "What was the first?"

"I met this kid in Wisconsin named Jeremy, and he told me this really strange story about werewolves."

Ryan and I gasped at the same time.

"Werewolves?" I said, my eyes wide.

"Werewolves?" Ryan repeated. "Like . . . *real* werewolves?"

Stephen nodded. "You want to hear about it?" he asked.

"Are you kidding?" I replied.

"Yeah!" Ryan exclaimed. "This I've got to hear!"

"Okay," Stephen said. "This is exactly what Jeremy told me . . . ."

Next:

#7: Wisconsin Werewolves

Continue on for a FREE preview!

Hide and seek. That's the game we were playing one night. The night that everything started to happen.

It's one of my favorite games to play, especially after dark. I'm great at finding places to hide.

There were six of us playing on this particular night. Sometimes there's as many as twelve, which can be really fun.

But tonight wasn't going to be much fun. Oh, it started out fun . . . but that's not the way it ended up.

"Jeremy!"

My mom's voice echoed down the block and through the small forest where we were playing. We'd been outside for a couple of hours, and the sun had just set. It would be really dark soon, and then it would be a *lot* of fun.

"Jeremy!"

Drats. That was the second time. When Mom calls, I'm supposed to holler back so she knows where I'm at. Problem is, if I yelled now, Colette might find me. She was 'it', and I could hear her searching in the forest not far from where I was hiding.

"Jeremy! Answer me!"

I had no choice. If I didn't answer Mom, she'd come looking for me. Then I'd *really* be in trouble.

"I'm fine Mom!" I shouted out the words as quickly as I could. I hoped that I didn't give away my hiding place to Colette!

"Thirty more minutes!" Mom hollered back. Then I heard our front door close.

Well, I thought, *I'm sure Colette heard me. I just hope she couldn't hear me well enough to find out where I was hiding.*

And I was hiding in a pretty good spot, I must admit. I found a spruce tree that had branches growing all the way to the ground, and I climbed within the thick, prickly limbs and hunkered to the ground as close as I possibly could. I knew that if I could just stay quiet, Colette would never find me here.

Crunch. Crunch-crunch.

I could hear Colette getting closer and closer. I knew she'd heard me, but I was hidden really well.

Crunch. Ker-snap.

She'd stepped on a branch, and stopped.

This is too cool, I thought. She was only a few feet away, but she would never find me here!

An owl hooted from far off. A mosquito buzzed by my ear. Stars began twinkling in the rapidly-coming night.

Crunch.

Colette took a step, and, for the first time, I could see her silhouette in the shadows. She wasn't far away at all. I just needed to sit tight and not make a sound.

Then I heard a voice from farther away:
"Tag! You're it!"

It was Colette . . . but that was impossible!
Colette was standing just a few feet in front of me!

I could hear the crunch and snap of twigs as
others emerged from their hiding places — but the
figure in front of me didn't move. I must have
mistaken someone else for Colette.

I pushed a branch away, and the needles
scraped my arm as I stood up.

"I knew she'd never find me," I said to the
person standing near. "That's a great hiding spot,
there."

Whoever it was, they didn't speak. Instead, I
heard a sniffing sound, like a dog that has picked
up the scent of something.

"Who are you?" I asked, knowing that it could
only be one of four other friends who were
playing hide and seek.

No answer.

"Hey, suit yourself," I said, and I began
walking away . . . until I heard a low growl.

"Funny," I said, pulling out a small flashlight

from my pocket. "Real funny." I clicked on the flashlight, shined it directly into the face of whoever it was . . . and received the shock of my life. The figure before me wasn't one of my friends. It had a hairy face, and a long, sharp nose. Long fangs dripped over the edges of his mouth, and its black eyes glowed an eerie yellow in the gleam of the flashlight.

Right then and there, I knew what it was.

I was face to face — with a werewolf.

I screamed and spun at the same time. I had to get away, and fast.

"*Ahhhhhhgggggghhhhh!!!*" I screamed as I ran through the brush. Branches whipped at my face and scratched at my arms. Limbs reached out like spiny arms, and I nearly tripped and fell.

"*Jeremy!*" I heard Colette call out. "*Where are you?!?! What's the matter?!?!*"

"I'm here!" I shouted. "Help me!"

I found the trail that weaves through the woods, and ran lickety-split, fast as my legs would carry me, toward our home base. Actually, it's just a small clearing in the woods where we all gather to begin our games of hide and seek.

I ran and ran, not chancing to look behind me for fear of seeing the dark figure of the werewolf coming after me. I'd heard that werewolves were really fast, and I didn't want to take any chances.

It was growing darker and darker, and I didn't notice the figures coming toward me on the trail until it was too late. I smacked into someone dead-on, and we both went flying, along with two people that were right behind him. I heard Colette gasp as she hit the ground, and then Tyler Norris. Colette and Tyler are two of my best friends.

"Jeremy!" Tyler said as he rolled on the ground. "What's the matter?!?!?"

"Run!" I said, getting to my feet. "There's a werewolf after me!"

"What?!?!" Tyler replied. "You're nutty like a fruitcake!"

"What are you talking about?" Colette asked.

By now, I had gotten to my feet again. I was staring back down the trail, trying to see if there was any movement. It was too dark to tell.

"I'm telling you, I saw a werewolf back there," I repeated, still gasping for breath. "I thought it was Colette, but it wasn't."

"Sure," Brian Ludwig mocked. "A werewolf. Yeah, they're all over the place. Gotta watch out for them werewolves."

"I'm serious, you guys!"

The rest of the group had gathered around. There was Tyler, Colette, Brian, Stuart Lester, James Barker, and me. We all live on the same block, just a few houses from one another.

"Jeremy, there's no such thing as werewolves," Colette said. "You probably saw a coyote."

"Hey, if coyotes stand as tall as you on their hind legs, well, then maybe it *was* a coyote," I answered.

"You're making this up," Stuart said.

"Look, you guys," I said. I was getting angry. "I know what I saw. I saw a creature that was about my size. It was standing on its hind legs, just like a human. Except it had hair all over its face, and it had a dog-like nose. And teeth! Man, did that thing have sharp teeth!"

"Was it really ugly?" James asked.

"Yeah!" I replied.

"Nasty looking?"

"Uh-huh."

"So ugly that you thought you would puke?"

"Yes! Exactly!" I said.

"That settles it, then," James said, matter-of-factly. "That was no werewolf . . . that was my *sister!*"

Everyone started laughing, except Colette and me. "Come on, you guys," she said. "Jeremy really saw something. He's not lying."

"No, I'm not," I said.

"Well, then . . . let's go see if he's still there," Tyler suggested.

Silence.

"Yeah," I said. "Unless you guys are chicken."

"I'm not afraid of any werewolf," Stuart said.

"Me neither," James said.

"Doesn't bother me a bit," Brian chimed in.

"Yeah," said Colette. "The six of us will be safe together. Let's go and see."

I pointed my flashlight beam down the trail, and eerie shadows darted and dove.

"We'll follow you," Stuart said, pulling out his own flashlight. Colette turned her flashlight on, and so did Brian, Tyler, and Stuart. We were six kids with six flashlights, heading down a trail that led into the forest.

Looking for a werewolf.

What we didn't know, of course, was that the werewolf was looking for *us*.

We walked down the trail, each of us sweeping our flashlights into the dark forest around us. Bats chittered as they darted through the trees, and I heard the owl hoot again. That's one of the things I like about Madison, Wisconsin, which is where I live. It's a pretty big city, but we live a little way out, and there are lots of forests and trees right near our neighborhood. Which means that there are plenty of animals, too. You'll see deer and racoons and owls . . . all kinds of wildlife

But you're not supposed to see werewolves.

Werewolves aren't supposed to be real.

"Are you sure you saw a werewolf?" Brian asked, as we trudged along the trail. "I mean . . . couldn't it have been a bear or something?"

I shook my head. "No way," I replied. "I'm telling you guys . . . I know what I saw. Come on, you know me . . . I'm not making this up. I really was scared. That thing was freaky."

"How much farther do we have to go?" James whined. "I'm missing *SpongeBob,* you know."

"Chill out, James," Colette said. "Your dad is probably recording the show, anyway. He likes it more than you do."

"Well, if we don't find the werewolf soon, I'm going to have to bag it for the night," Brian said. "I've got to get up early to go fishing."

"Awww, is the little baby getting tired?" Stuart chided. Brian ignored the comment.

And the trail wound on. By now, it was really dark. There was no moon, but a zillion stars glistened through the trees.

"See?" Stuart said, pointing his thin flashlight beam up into the air. "It couldn't have been a werewolf. Werewolves only come out when the moon is full."

"That's just an old wives' tale," Tyler said. "Werewolves can come out at any time."

And then I heard something. It was a crunching, a snapping of branches, and the sound wasn't too far away from us. Stuart heard it, and so did Colette.

The six of us stopped in the middle of the trail, listening. The noise had stopped, and all we could hear were the sounds of the forest.

And then:

Crunch. Snap.

We froze stiff. None of us spoke or even moved.

But there was only silence. Whatever it was, it wasn't moving around much.

Colette leaned toward me and started to whisper. *"Is this the place where you —"*

But her voice was stopped cold by a shrill, new sound.

A howl.

It was long and loud, and it echoed through

the forest . . . and there was no mistaking it.

That howl—that awful, screeching wail—wasn't from a dog or an owl. In fact, no human could make a sound like that.

That howl was from a werewolf.

And when we heard the crunching of branches and the snapping of twigs, I knew that we would never get out of the forest alive.

I suppose you think that we turned and ran.

Wrong.

We *flew*. I don't think our feet hit the ground. We turned and sprang so quickly that we bounced off one another, careening down the dark trail like wild banshees. All of us were screaming . . . even Colette, who usually doesn't scream about anything.

We ran and we screamed, we screamed and we ran. We tore through the dark forest, following our flashlight beams as they bounced along the trail, trying to put as much distance between us and the ghastly creature that, no doubt, was hot on our trail. And we didn't stop until we reached the edge of the forest and the safety of streetlights that glowed brightly along our block.

When we reached the street, all six of us collapsed, sitting on the curb and gasping for air. It was a long time before anyone said anything.

"I'm sorry, Jeremy," Tyler said. "I should have believed you."

"Me too," said James. The rest of the group nodded.

"That was the freakiest sound I've ever heard in my life," Brian said between his heaving gasps. "I didn't think we were going to make it out of there. Not alive, anyway."

"That's what I was trying to tell you guys," I said. "Whatever is in those woods . . . whether it's a werewolf or not . . . isn't human."

"You can bet it's not a cartoon, either," Stuart said, which prompted mild laughter from everyone.

"So . . . what do we do now?" Colette said, pulling a lock of hair away from her face.

"I don't know about you guys," James said, "but I'm going to go home and forget the whole thing. I'm going to wake up in the morning, and this whole thing will be a dream. There's no such thing as werewolves, anyway."

We all sat on the curb, catching our breath. Above us, bugs swarmed and darted beneath the pale blue streetlight.

I would have liked to think that James was right. It would have been great to wake up and discover that everything was a dream, that we hadn't even been in the woods playing hide and seek.

But that's not what happened.

Soon, I would discover—with absolute certainty—that what had happened to us was *real*.

And as I sat on the curb that night with my friends, I wondered about werewolves. I wondered if they really did exist. I wondered if I would ever see the creature again . . . and if I wanted to.

I didn't have to wait very long . . . for the werewolf had followed us. We didn't know it at the time, but the werewolf had crept through the shadows and was watching us at that very moment.

We were safe, of course, because we were under the glow of the streetlight.

But later that night, after I went to bed, I heard a noise outside my window. I got up to investigate . . . and what I saw sends shivers of terror down my spine to this very day.

ABOUT THE AUTHOR

Johnathan Rand is the author of more than 65 books, with well over 4 million copies in print. Series include **AMERICAN CHILLERS, MICHIGAN CHILLERS, FREDDIE FERNORTNER, FEARLESS FIRST GRADER,** and **THE ADVENTURE CLUB.** He's also co-authored a novel for teens (with Christopher Knight) entitled **PANDEMIA.** When not traveling, Rand lives in northern Michigan with his wife and three dogs. He is also the only author in the world to have a store that sells only his works: **CHILLERMANIA!** is located in Indian River, Michigan. Johnathan Rand is not always at the store, but he has been known to drop by frequently. Find out more at:

www.americanchillers.com

Also by Johnathan Rand:

GHOST IN THE GRAVEYARD

FUN FACTS ABOUT ILLINOIS:

State Capitol: Springfield

Became a state in 1818

State Insect: Monarch Butterfly

State Bird: Cardinal

State Animal: White-Tailed Deer

State Tree: White Oak

State Fish: Bluegill

State Flower: Purple Violet

State Slogan: 'Land of Lincoln'

The total area of Illinois is 56,400 square miles!

FAMOUS PEOPLE FROM ILLINOIS!

Abraham Lincoln, 16th President of the United States

Michael Jordan, basketball player.

John Deere, who first introduced the steel plow to Illinois

Oprah Winfrey, television personality

Benny Goodman, musician and band leader

among many others!

Johnathan Rand travels internationally
for school visits and book signings! For
booking information, call:

1 (231) 238-0338!

www.americanchillers.com

Join the official

AMERICAN
CHILLERS

FAN CLUB!

Visit www.americanchillers.com for details

All AudioCraft books are proudly printed, bound, and manufactured in the United States of America, utilizing American resources, labor, and materials.

USA